Acting Edition

I0584673

LA RUTA

by Isaac Gómez

FOR PRODUCTION INQUIRIES

UNITED STATES AND CANADA
info@concordtheatricals.com
1-866-979-0447

UNITED KINGDOM AND EUROPE
licensing@concordtheatricals.co.uk
020-7054-7298

Each title is subject to availability from Concord Theatricals Corp., depending upon country of performance. Please be aware that LA RUTA may not be licensed by Concord Theatricals Corp. in your territory. Professional and amateur producers should contact the nearest Concord Theatricals Corp. office or licensing partner to verify availability.

LA RUTA was first produced by Steppenwolf Theatre Company (Artistic Director Anna D. Shapiro; Executive Director David Schmitz) in Chicago, Illinois, and opened on December 20, 2018.

The performance was directed by Steppenwolf Ensemble Member Sandra Marquez, featuring Steppenwolf Ensemble Member Karen Rodriguez, with dramaturgy and new play development by Polly Hubbard, scenic design by Regina García, costume design by Christine Pascual, lighting design by Jesse Klug, sound design by Mikhail Fiksel, projection design by Rasean Davonte Johnson, music direction by Zacbe Pichardo, vocal direction by Andra Velis Simon, fight choreography by Gaby Labotka, music development by Laura Crotte, and casting by JC Clementz. The company voice and text coach was Gigi Buffington, and the assistant to the playwright was Brenna Barborka. The production stage manager was Christine D. Freeburg, with assistant stage manager Amanda Landis. The cast was as follows:

YOLI . . . . Sandra Delgado

MARISELA. . . . . Charín Álvarez

IVONNE. . . . . Karen Rodriguez

BRENDA . . . . Cher Álvarez

ZAIDE. . . . . Mari Marroquin

DESAMAYA. . . . . Laura Crotte

WOMEN OF JUÁREZ . . . . Alice da Cunha & Isabella Gerasole

CHARACTERS

YOLI – a mother, 40s

MARISELA – a mother, 40s

IVONNE – a friend, 26

BRENDA – a daughter, 16

ZAIDE – a maquila worker, 40s

DESAMAYA – a singer/musician who is both timeless and ageless, any age

WOMEN OF JUÁREZ – women who fill the world of Juárez, all ages (could be two women, could be twenty, depending on needs of production.)

All the characters are Mexican and should be cast accordingly. The greater the intergenerational difference between the women, the better.

SETTING

Ciudad Juárez, Mexico

TIME

Various months throughout 1998 and 2000

MUSIC

Music in the play should not feel separate from it, but a character in and of itself. Desamaya is built into the script as our rebar in how music works in this world, so it's appropriate that she be the conduit into how we experience music as well. She plays a guitar throughout the show and she is good. Like, really, really good. Like bone-chilling, of the earth, goosebumps in her *ays* good. She's considered *la reina de Juárez* for a reason. Sheet music to songs can be made available upon request.

"El Son del Obrero" is written by Gabino Palomares and "Siete Soles" is written by Rafael Mendoza. Both have given permission for these songs to be included with the script, so long as credit is given during the production. It is their gift for the activism of the play, and I am profoundly grateful for that gift.

"La Bruja" and "Cielito Lindo" are public domain. See separate page on music for more information on the songs themselves.

TRANSITIONS

The play is structured non-linearly because that's the world these women live in. The information they receive is non-linear, changes constantly, and is often in contradiction with itself. And with each and every day a new discovery feels a lot like whiplash and the audience's experience of the structure of the play should reflect that.

Because the play bounces back and forth in time, it is crucial that transitions help communicate our time and place. Scene headers in bold should be projected onto the walls, and Desamaya playing songs that tonally linger momentarily in the scene before, or gradually take us into the scene we're about to experience, will help immensely.

Use Selena with caution and intention, but please try to use her. I highly recommend "Amor Prohibido" between scenes seven and eight. The audience and the cast will need it. For further information, please see the Music and Third-Party Materials Use Note on page iii.

A NOTE ON LIFE

This piece doesn't have the typical emotional trajectory as a standard play but it rather lives in a space where emotion comes crashing and then becomes immediately still. The women in Juárez aren't crying every moment of every day and this play, though dark and heavy at times, should reflect this. I highly encourage exploring levity in moments where it feels very heavy, and staying away from tears unless indicated in the script.

LANGUAGE

A slash [/] indicates the start place for the following line.

A number [1] beside a forward slash [/] indicates the start place for the line that follows the number.

Spanish in the play is indicated with *italics*. It is not an indication of emphasis. CAPS and underlines do that.

CONTINUE THE JOURNEY

LA RUTA is the sister play to *THE WAY SHE SPOKE.* I highly recommend reading both. Perhaps consider programming them in rep as these two sister plays are inextricably connected. They speak to each other. Although I wrote *LA RUTA* before *THE WAY SHE SPOKE,* they both speak to ongoing systemic violence against women and femmes in Juárez and beyond; these two plays are two sides of the same coin, illuminating a holistic interrogation and excavation of these women's stories. To this day, I still do not know why the brave and bold women represented in the play you are about to read have trusted me with their stories. I only aspire to be a vessel in hopes that one day, dear reader, one of you might know what to do to stop all this.

THE MUSIC OF *LA RUTA*

The songs of *LA RUTA* derive from a variety of sources: classic Mexican folk songs, and contemporary protest songs. Below are some histories and context for the music in this play.

(Original Translations by Itzel Blancas.)

"El Son del Obrero (Worker's Song)"
...You are a worker and I am one too,
If we remain separated there will never be a revolution...
...I'm in search of a new world without borders and no boss...

Written by Gabino Palomares (one of the main exponents of the Nueva Cancíon movement in Latin America – a social movement and musical genre characterized by folk-inspired styles and socially committed lyrics), this migrant worker's song (and songs like this one) played a profound role in the social upheavals in Latin America during the 1970s and 1980s ("El Son del Obrero" was released in 1975). In the context of maquila (factory) workers in Ciudad Juárez, the song is re-contextualized to encompass the 255,000 people (mostly women) who work directly in Juárez's 330 maquiladoras approximately twelve hours per day, making an average of fifty cents per day, and under some of the most challenging work conditions globally – all for U.S. export. Many of the women who are kidnapped live in poverty; many of them work at the maquilas.

"Cielito Lindo (Lovely Sweet One)"
...Sing and don't cry,
Because singing brightens,
Lovely sky, the hearts.
That beauty mark you have,
Lovely sky, next to your lips,
Don't give it to anyone,
Lovely sky, because it is mine...

"Cielito Lindo" is a popular Mexican song popularized in 1882 by Mexican author Quirino Mendoza y Cortés and is commonly played by Mariachi bands – often sung by men. "Cielito Lindo" roughly translates to "Lovely Sweet One," functioning as a term of endearment comparable to sweetheart or honey and is emblematic of resilience and celebration amidst incomparable grief and loss (an evolution of a song originating in possessiveness of men over women throughout the centuries.) In the context of *LA RUTA* and sung by women in Juárez, the "sweet one" refers to missing daughters, the yearning for them by their mothers, and pushing through the most unspeakable of losses. This song is a Mexican staple.

"*Siete Soles* (Seven Suns)"

...The desert only dried my tears
The darkness only killed my dreams
I was only following the lure of a mirage
Beneath the seven suns
I fell into the abyss...

Originally written and performed by Rafael Mendoza for the original film *7 Soles*, this song characterizes a migration to the United States from Mexico and Latin America and is traditionally performed in the style of *canto cardenche* – Mexico's most haunting musical style – which is traditionally sung by men. The word "cardenche" refers to a desert cactus plant with painful, prickly thorns paralleling how canto cardenche focuses on pain, both emotional and physical. The lyrics also describe the hardships of desert life and lost loves. Death above all is an ever-present theme in the genre, which is also true when song in the context of *LA RUTA*, and the missing and murdered women of Juárez.

"*La Bruja* (The Witch)"

The witch takes hold of me,
She takes me to her house...
...Oh tell me? Tell me? Oh why don't you tell me?
How many little ones have you sucked dry?

One of the oldest traditional Mexican folk songs with many conflicting origin stories, "La Bruja" originates in the state of Veracruz though has been popularized and re-contextualized in various musical genre styles throughout the rest of Mexico. There are a number of stories and legends of ghosts, demons and witches in some rural areas of Mexico, and "La Bruja" is sung to warn and scare young children to behave or the witch will take you and suck out your soul. In the context of *LA RUTA*, "La Bruja" challenges the notion that women in Juárez are magically disappearing when in actuality, these women are being kidnapped, and the perpetuators of this violence are very real, they aren't magical creatures but are treated by government officials and authorities as if they were – unable to be caught and held accountable for their crimes.

For all the roses in Juárez –
the missing and the lost,
the survivors and the ones left behind.
Para todas.
Para siempre.

For Bianca, for showing me the light when I was stuck in the dark;
For Genesis, for showing me the way every time I got lost;
For Andrea, for the prayer when it snowed;
For Blanca and her mother, the guides before sunset;
For Karen, the fire in the cold that never burns out;

For every woman who has ever touched this play & who will ever touch
this play: the messengers, the torch-carriers, the ones who yell from the
top of the Guadalupe mountains;

And for Yolanda. Always for Yolanda. Always.

One
La Bruja and 1:20 a.m

(A bus stop somewhere in Ciudad Juárez, Mexico.)

(The only nearby light source is an old wooden streetlight/telephone wire pole that flickers on and off every now and again.)

(Painted on the pole is a pink square with a black cross laced carefully in its center – also run down from rain and sand in the wind.)

(Leaning against the lamppost is a woman with a guitar. A singer. Her name is **DESAMAYA.** *She's been here many times before.)*

(The sound of a bus stopping. Women dressed in maquila uniforms hop off and quickly make their way home.)

(As the light on the lamppost flickers, **DESAMAYA** *watches them leave. She strums on her guitar and sings.)*

[I. "LA BRUJA"]

DESAMAYA.
¡AY QUÉ BONITO ES VOLAR
A LAS DOS DE LA MAÑANA!
¡AY QUÉ BONITO ES VOLAR
EN LOS BRAZOS DE TU HERMANA, AY MAMÁ!

ME AGARRA LA BRUJA,
ME LLEVA A SU CASA,
ME VUELVE MACETA,
Y UNA CALABAZA
ME AGARRA LA BRUJA,
ME LLEVA AL CERRITO,
ME VUELVE MACETA,
Y UN CALABACITO
¡AY! DÍGAME, Y DÍGAME, Y DÍGAME USTED,
¿CUÁNTAS CREATURITAS SE HA CHUPADO USTED?
NINGUNA, NINGUNA, NINGUNA NO VÉ,
QUE ANDO EN PRETENSIONES DE CHUPARME A USTED.

> *(A moment.)*

> *(Then, as* **DESAMAYA** *disappears into the shadows,* **MARISELA** *and* **YOLANDA** *can be seen sitting on a bench.* **MARISELA** *holds a stack of fliers in her hands. She's in the middle of telling* **YOLANDA** *a story. The most hilarious kind.)*

> *(Projections:* **TUESDAY JULY 7, 1998. 1:20 A.M.***)*

MARISELA. *(Laughing.)* Where *is* Yesenia anyway?

YOLANDA. *(Laughing, coming down.)* Day shift pick up.

MARISELA. Oh.

> *(A moment.)*

Y Marisol?

YOLANDA. Day shift.

MARISELA. Oh.

> *(A moment.)*

At least it's nice tonight, no?

YOLANDA. Mhmm. Very clear.

MARISELA. *(Pointing.)* It's a new moon, *mira*.

YOLANDA. It's so dark. Can barely see a thing.

MARISELA. Yeah but she's still there. She's just acting shy.

YOLANDA. Why do they call it that? New moon.

> *(Beat.)*

MARISELA. That's a good question.

> *(**MARISELA** pulls out a wrinkled scrap piece of paper and a pen from her purse and writes it down.)*

YOLANDA. *Qué estás haciendo, bebita?*

MARISELA. Every time I hear a question I can't answer, I write it down.

> *(Beat.)*

Like this one here, *mira*.

> *(Reading, serious, in awe.)*

"What if God was one of us?"

That's a good one, right?

YOLANDA. Mari you stole that from that song.

MARISELA. What song?

YOLANDA. That song on *la radio*, you know which one.

MARISELA. I don't know what you're talking about.

YOLANDA. Mhmm.

MARISELA. I heard it from a *mujer* in *El Centro*.

YOLANDA. I'm sure you did.

MARISELA. Seriously! She was running around *toda loca* with her *chichis* out in the open, waving her bra in the air smelling like *caca* yelling, "what if God was one of us?!" I stopped and thought, "Hm. That's a good question."

YOLANDA. *(Laughing.) Ay mujer,* you need to be careful with that stuff.

MARISELA. It's not like I'm hanging out with her or anything. I was just putting up some fliers. *Mira.* I tried a new picture this time.

(**MARISELA** *shows* **YOLANDA** *one of her fliers.*)

This one's from her *quince. Qué bonita, no?*

YOLANDA. *Sí.* I remember that day like it was yesterday.

MARISELA. It almost feels like it, huh. See this picture is clearer, no? I thought the other one was too grainy.

YOLANDA. *Pues sí.*

MARISELA. You can see the dimple on her cheek.

YOLANDA. You can. It's right there.

MARISELA. She's beautiful, *verdad*?

YOLANDA. Mhmm. Just like her mother.

(*A moment.*)

(*Beat.*)

(*Beat.*)

(*Beat.*)

(*Beat.*)

It's getting colder no?

MARISELA. You're cold?

YOLANDA. I'm freezing.

MARISELA. It's July.

YOLANDA. It's the desert.

MARISELA. I'm hot. Can't stop sweating.

> (*Beat.*)

I think I'm having hot flashes.

YOLANDA. No you're not.

MARISELA. I am, I am. I'm / sure of it.

YOLANDA. Mari, you're younger than me.

MARISELA. No I'm not.

YOLANDA. Yes you are. You're –

MARISELA. Ahp ahp ahp! You gotta whisper these things. Can't have my secrets out there in these streets like that. *A ver, dime.*

> (**YOLANDA** *whispers a year in* **MARI***'s ear.*)

Nope.

YOLANDA. But if I'm...you told me you...that's impossible, you *have* to be.

MARISELA. Yeah... I lied.

YOLANDA. What?!

MARISELA. When we first met, I lied. But then so many years passed and I started to believe it myself.

> (*They laugh.*)

YOLANDA. How old are you then?

> (**MARISELA** *whispers her age in* **YOLANDA***'s ear.*)

No you're not.

MARISELA. Yolanda, why would I lie about that?

YOLANDA. You've been lying for years. Who's to say you're not lying now?

MARISELA. Seriously, I'm not lying *this* time.

(**YOLANDA** *bursts into laughter.*)

What?! I'm not!

YOLANDA. *Ay, Marisela.* You're going to be the death of me, you know that?

> (**MARISELA** *laughs with her. Grabs* **YOLANDA***'s hand in hers.*)

MARISELA. And you'll be the death of me, too.

> (*A moment. Two friends enjoying each other.*)
>
> (*Then.*)
>
> (*The sound of a bus stopping and fierce headlights shine on.*)

YOLANDA. *(Quiet.)* Alright. Go ahead. Good luck.

> (*Several women hop out of the vehicle dressed in maquila uniforms. As they pass the two women seated on the bench,* **MARISELA** *hands each of them a flier.* **YOLANDA** *looks hard for someone.*)

MARISELA. *Disculpen senoritas,* have you seen my daughter? Here is her picture. Her name is Rubí. She has dark hair and brown eyes...she looks just like you.

> (*Beat.*)
>
> (**MARISELA** *has freaked them out. The young women leave in a quickness.*)

Wait, that's not what I –

Esperen. ESPEREN!

> (*And just like that, they are gone.*)

(*To* **YOLANDA***.*) How was that?

YOLANDA. You've gotta work on your interpersonal skills.

MARISELA. *Qué es eso* interpersonal skills. I'm very interpersonal.

YOLANDA. No, no of course you are. What I'm saying is you need to be more relatable.

MARISELA. It was easier when we practiced at home.

YOLANDA. You know what they say: practice makes perfect.

MARISELA. You think they heard me?

YOLANDA. Oh yeah.

MARISELA. Okay. Good.

> *(A moment.)*

> *(Then.)*

> *(The bus drives away. Brenda is nowhere to be found. The panic sets in like ice water on dry skin.)*

YOLANDA. Did you see Brenda?

MARISELA. No...

YOLANDA. Brenda was supposed to be on that bus. / 1:20 a.m.

MARISELA. Already?

Right.

> *(Beat.)*

Maybe she got off with Ivonne.

YOLANDA. No, no that's not like her. She always knows where I wait.

MARISELA. Okay, well then maybe she –

YOLANDA. *(More pressing.)* Marisela, she always knows where I wait.

MARISELA. Okay well maybe they all had to stay a little late. You know how José runs that factory. / *Hijo de puta.*

YOLANDA. I don't know, Mari, what if she's...what if she...

MARISELA. *Eh, eh, eh.* No. None of that. Okay?

There's one more bus coming any minute now. She's gotta be on that one. We can wait. We're already up.

  (A moment.)

Just breathe, *amorcita.*

YOLANDA. *Si. Si.* / Okay.

MARISELA. She's definitely on that one. I know it. We'll just wait.

  (They sit. They wait.)

  (Beat.)

  (Beat.)

  (Beat.)

YOLANDA. I hate the waiting.

  (Beat.)

MARISELA. I told you not to start her on the night shift, *pero* you / never listen.

YOLANDA. The money's better, she's making twice as much.

MARISELA. Have you seen it?

YOLANDA. What?

MARISELA. The extra money.

(Beat.)

YOLANDA. José said these things take time.

MARISELA. He also said our services were no longer needed, in / case you forgot.

YOLANDA. Don't take it personal, Mari. This is new, it's all new they're...figuring it out.

MARISELA. Kick the old women out, keep the young ones as / slaves.

YOLANDA. They didn't kick us out. *Que estas / diciendo?*

MARISELA. Wasn't that the point of this whole factory thing? *Sin fronteras?* Free trade, *o quien sabe.* What did they call it? NALGA?

YOLANDA. NAFTA.

MARISELA. *NAFTA. Psh. NAFTA mis nalgas.*

YOLANDA. Give it a chance, Mari. It's supposed to be good for us, good for all of us.

MARISELA. Ha!

YOLANDA. And the *maquilas* are a part of that. With all these U.S. companies building factories left and right? It's like...we finally have a shot here. To make our own money, support our own families.

(Beat.)

José said by the end of the month Brenda would be making more. He gave me his word.

MARISELA. Well I don't trust him.

YOLANDA. He's been really good to us, Mari. Really good.

MARISELA. He hasn't been good to me. He wasn't good to Rubí.

(Beat. A moment.)

YOLANDA. We don't know what actually happened to Rubí, Marisela, that's the thing.

MARISELA. Are you serious / right now?

YOLANDA. It could have been José. It could have also been her boyfriend, / it could have been anyone.

MARISELA. It wasn't.

YOLANDA. We don't know if José had anything to do with it. What if it's just / gossip –?

MARISELA. He was the last person to see her.

YOLANDA. Do you know that for sure?

MARISELA. Yes. Well, I don't – I wasn't there –

YOLANDA. You see? That's what I'm saying, Mari. You don't know if he had anything to do with it, and that's okay. / That's why the police are there.

MARISELA. As far as *mi niña* is concerned? He has everything to do with it. Everything.

YOLANDA. Fine. You're right. / Like always.

MARISELA. I'm going to find her, Yolanda. I am.

YOLANDA. I know. I / know.

MARISELA. Sick of this shit.

YOLANDA. I know.

It's just...

Brenda's never late.

>   (*Beat.*)

>   (*A moment.*)

>   (*Then.*)

>   (*The sound of another bus stopping. Again, several women hop out of the vehicle dressed*

in maquila uniforms. **MARISELA** *grabs* **YOLANDA**'s *hand as they stand and watch the last group of girls pass them by. Brenda is nowhere to be found.)*

(Beat.)

(Beat.)

(Beat.)

(Beat.)

MARISELA. Last one till dawn.

(A moment.)

YOLANDA. Marisela.

MARISELA. I know. I'll call the police.

(Lights shift.)

Two
Busses and Maquiladoras

(Projections: **MONDAY MAY 4, 1998. TWO MONTHS BEFORE BRENDA'S DISAPPEARANCE.***)*

(The inside of a maquiladora – a U.S.-owned factory.)

(The sounds of women working furiously at machines are heard. It is rhythmic and methodical – almost a song in and of itself.)

(The sound is never ending and is a mixture of sewing machines moving at a rapid speed and the sounds of large irons pressing into thick fabrics, waiting to be cut and distributed.)

(This goes on for awhile. "La Bruja" plays on the radio overhead. Not the same rhythm or tempo as when we first heard it. More like how you might hear it on a popular radio station.)

ZAIDE. *Oye!* Can somebody up there change the station please?

(Under her breath.) I fucking hate this song.

> *(Nothing. The women keep working, mumbling to themselves. "La Bruja" plays on.)*

(Playful.) Por favor, Señores, estamos sudando. Something with more of a beat. Keeps us quick.

(A moment.)

(Then.)

(Radio static for a short while, then the sounds of Spanish commercials, news, rancheras, reggaeton, banda, and more.)

Wait, wait go back! *(1)*

(The channel returns to a song with a familiar tune with a beat. Very Juareño, Norteño.)

Eso! I love this song! The sound of Desamaya's voice, listen...

(They listen to **DESAMAYA** *humming, riffing.)*

The voice of a *Norteña.*

(A grito escapes **ZAIDE***'s lips. The voice of a woman can be heard over the speakers.)*

[II. "EL SON DEL OBRERO"]

DESAMAYA.
(1) TRABAJADORA ERES TÚ TRABAJADORA TAMBIÉN YO,
TRABAJADORA ERES TÚ TRABAJADORA TAMBIÉN YO;
SI SEGUIMOS SEPARADAS NUNCA HABRÁ REVOLUCIÓN,
SI SEGUIMOS SEPARADAS NUNCA HABRÁ REVOLUCIÓN

*(***ZAIDE** *sings along.)*

DESAMAYA & ZAIDE.
TRABAJADORA ERES TÚ TRABAJADORA TAMBIÉN YO,
TRABAJADORA ERES TÚ TRABAJADORA TAMBIÉN YO
SI SEGUIMOS SEPARADAS NUNCA HABRÁ REVOLUCIÓN,
SI SEGUIMOS SEPARADAS NUNCA HABRÁ REVOLUCIÓN
CON LA HERRAMIENTA EN MIS MANOS CON UN LIBRO EN
MI OVEROL

(Then, as the women work, they join in.)

ALL.
> CON LA HERRAMIENTA EN MIS MANOS CON UN LIBRO EN
> MI OVEROL

DESAMAYA & ZAIDE.
> VOY EN POS DE UN MUNDO NUEVO SIN FRONTERAS NI
> PATRÓN

ALL.
> VOY EN POS DE UN MUNDO NUEVO SIN FRONTERAS NI
> PATRÓN

> *(They stop singing, they keep working.*
> **BRENDA** *comes into view, guided by* **IVONNE.**
> **ZAIDE** *works furiously at her station. The*
> *music continues beneath them.)*

IVONNE. That's the grand tour. Here's where you'll be working. I'm right over here if you need anything.

BRENDA. So...that's it?

IVONNE. That's it.

BRENDA. *Pero –*

IVONNE. We work here, we eat over there, bathroom's down the hall. Not much else to it.

BRENDA. It looks a lot bigger from outside.

IVONNE. So does a *ranchero's* dick.

ZAIDE. You know everyone can hear you *cochina.*

IVONNE. It's true.

ZAIDE. *Pinche sucia.*

IVONNE. Don't get all butt hurt 'cause you look like a *pinche chola* and can't get none.

ZAIDE. Ha! Don't make me <u>spit.</u>

IVONNE. If you'd let me give you a makeover your eyebrows wouldn't be bigger than my hand Zaide.

ZAIDE. I wouldn't want you touching me if you were my last shot out of this *pinche cagadero.*

IVONNE. You wanna say that to my face, *puta*?

ZAIDE. *Calmate* I'm just messin' with you.

IVONNE. Bite me bitch.

ZAIDE. If you don't watch that mouth, / you're gonna end up like Azucena, *puta*.

IVONNE. What?

BRENDA. Who's / Azucena?

IVONNE. At least Azucena got all her shit done on time. You're getting slow, Zaide.

ZAIDE. No I'm not.

BRENDA. *(More pressing.)* Who's Azucena?

IVONNE. Aren't you scared? I'd be scared. You're one fuck up away from being outta here.

ZAIDE. You're not the boss here, / Ivonne.

BRENDA. *(More pressing.)* Who's Azucena?!

IVONNE. She used to work here, but she doesn't / anymore.

ZAIDE. She was kidnapped, Ivonne, / don't act like you don't know what happened to her.

IVONNE. No she wasn't.

BRENDA. *Mi mamá* said that's not gonna happen to me. I'm smart.

IVONNE. Yeah / *(1)* I see that. I can tell. *(2)*

ZAIDE. *(1)* So was she.

> *(2)* Weren't you friends with her? Weren't you with her when she went missing?

IVONNE. She didn't go missing. She works across / the street.

ZAIDE. I coulda sworn I saw you with her, y'all used to hang out or something like that?

IVONNE. You're old, Zaide. You didn't see shit.

ZAIDE. And what about Judíth? From RCA?

IVONNE. Who's Judíth?

ZAIDE. Don't give me that shit, you know who Judíth is. Tall. *Morena.*

> (*Beat.*)

IVONNE. What is this, a witch hunt?

ZAIDE. I just think it's interesting that every time a girl goes missing, you happen to be around, that's all.

> (*Beat.*)

IVONNE. *Cabróna!*

> (**IVONNE** *rushes her, tries to claw her eyes out, pulls her hair. The other girls hold her back.*)

BRENDA. Hey, hey! That's enough! *Ya parale!*

> (**ZAIDE** *retreats.*)

IVONNE. (*Fixing her hair, her eyebrows.*) Crazy dumbass bitch.

> (**ZAIDE** *goes back to work.*)

ZAIDE. Whatever.

IVONNE. That's right, keep my name out of your mouth 'cause you don't know shit, Zaide, YOU DON'T KNOW SHIT!

> (*Beat.*)

> (*To* **BRENDA.***)* You ready to try this thing or what?

(**BRENDA** *nods her head. The women keep working.*)

(*It is a repetitive motion of placing garments and fabrics on a small square machine, fitting them precisely in place, closing the lid, pushing down hard, and slowly releasing before opening the machine, removing the fabric, and beginning the process all over again.*)

(**BRENDA** *is lost. Through observation of the other women, she attempts the routine herself but can't keep up with their pace.*)

ALL.
CUIDARÉ LAS HERRAMIENTAS Y CON ELLAS TE HE DE DAR
CUIDARÉ LAS HERRAMIENTAS Y CON ELLAS TE HE DE DAR
NO MÁS GANANCIAS AL AMO TODO A LA COMUNIDAD
NO MÁS GANANCIAS AL AMO TODO A LA COMUNIDAD
TRABAJADORA ERES TU TRABAJADORA TAMBIÉN YO,
TRABAJADORA ERES TU TRABAJADORA TAMBIÉN YO
SI SEGUIMOS SEPARADAS NUNCA HABRÁ REVOLUCIÓN,
SI SEGUIMOS SEPARADAS NUNCA HABRÁ REVOLUCIÓN
MI CUERPO LO CONVIRTIERON EN CARNE DE
    EXPLOTACIÓN
MI CUERPO LO CONVIRTIERON EN CARNE DE
    EXPLOTACIÓN
POR DIGNIFICAR LA HISTORIA TOMAREMOS EL TIMÓN
POR DIGNIFICAR LA HISTORIA TOMAREMOS EL TIMÓN
POCO A POCO DESPERTANDO MAÑANA SEREMOS MÁS
POCO A POCO DESPERTANDO MAÑANA SEREMOS MÁS
LA REVOLUCIÓN EXIGE SER LEVADURA DEL PAN
LA REVOLUCIÓN EXIGE SER LEVADURA DEL PAN
TRABAJADORA ERES TÚ TRABAJADORA TAMBIÉN YO,
TRABAJADORA ERES TÚ TRABAJADORA TAMBIÉN YO;
SI SEGUIMOS SEPARADAS NUNCA HABRÁ REVOLUCIÓN,
SI SEGUIMOS SEPARADAS NUNCA HABRÁ REVOLUCIÓN

(The sound of a buzzer is heard, signaling the first of two ten minute breaks. The women breathe, grunt, stretch. One by one, they clock out, leaving **BRENDA** *and* **IVONNE** *alone.)*

BRENDA. What was that? Wait, where's everyone going?

IVONNE. First break. Bathroom lines get long, so.

BRENDA. Oh then I should probably –

*(***IVONNE*** notices the mess at Brenda's work station.)*

IVONNE. You have no idea what you're doing, do you.

BRENDA. That obvious, huh?

IVONNE. Here. Let me help. We got ten minutes, come on, let's go.

*(***IVONNE*** takes over Brenda's work station and shows her how to operate the machine.)*

You gotta spin it around, fast, like this, *mira.*

(She preps. And she goes. She's really, really, fast.)

One. Two. Three. And out, onto the next one.

Es muy fácil. You try.

*(***BRENDA*** tries, but is a little slow and awkward with her hands.)*

One...

Two...

*(***BRENDA*** can't keep up with the pace.)*

And...out.

(A moment.)

You gotta be a lot faster than that *niña.*

BRENDA. I think I'll be okay.

(*Beat.*)

IVONNE. If you start falling asleep, give yourself a little pinch. I've seen a lot of fingers come in and out of this machine.

BRENDA. (*Sheer horror.*) WHAT?!

(**IVONNE** *laughs.*)

IVONNE. You're funny. Yolanda told me you were gonna be funny but like. You're really funny.

BRENDA. (*Awkward.*) Thanks.

IVONNE. Brenda, right?

BRENDA. Right.

IVONNE. Your mom talked about you *constantly*. God, it's been like a million years since I've seen her. How's she doing, is she good?

BRENDA. Yeah she's great.

IVONNE. See that machine over there? That's where she worked.

BRENDA. Oh wow, cool! Can I use that one?

IVONNE. No! It's busted. Like bitches hands be cut off and shit.

BRENDA. Oh wow.

IVONNE. Yeah Yolanda's a badass. I miss having her around. All these other *putas* are too much drama.

BRENDA. Why do you look so familiar? You sure we haven't met before?

IVONNE. Oh, I'm sure.

(*Beat. A realization.*)

Oh, you know what? I went to your *quince,* that's probably what it is.

BRENDA. YOU WENT TO MY QUINCE?!

IVONNE. Yeah.

BRENDA. *(Shocked.)* Why?

IVONNE. *(Laughing.)* Because Yolanda invited me...?

Well, she invited like everyone at the *maquila* but I'm the only who showed up.

BRENDA. Oh.

IVONNE. Like I said. *Putas.*

I was wearing the, uh –

BRENDA. Oh my god. / OH MY GOD.

IVONNE. What? *Que?!*

BRENDA. That was *you!* In the tight white floor length lace?

IVONNE. Yup, that was me. Yoli hated that I came in white.

(She laughs.)

BRENDA. You couldn't have picked any other color?

IVONNE. Hell no, I'm royalty bitch.

*(****BRENDA*** *laughs.)*

BRENDA. You looked hot.

IVONNE. Why thank you.

BRENDA. I remember looking at you thinking, "damn, she looks hot."

IVONNE. *Ay gracias! (Playful.) Síguele, síguele!*

You looked pretty good too.

(Beat.)

BRENDA. Really? That, that's what you thought?

IVONNE. *Como una princesa.*

BRENDA. *(Disappointed.)* Oh. I was actually going for something a little more like...well...a little more like you.

>*(Beat.)*

Well, not *you* exactly but just a little more like, I dunno... / Selena?

IVONNE. Selena?

>*(They gasp at having said Selena at the same time. A moment of true connection.)*

>*(The two laugh. A true friendship bond forming.)*

BRENDA. Yeah, see I knew you loved Selena, I was looking at your hair, / and I was like, "does she love Selena?"

IVONNE. Right, right. Same. I mean, well not really, / you know what I mean –

BRENDA. Right.

IVONNE. Right.

>*(Beat.)*

BRENDA. Why didn't you come say hi? At my *quince,* I mean.

IVONNE. You were busy being adored by everyone? Besides, I didn't stay long. Just a quick hello to Yolanda and to give her your gift.

>*(Sees **BRENDA**'s hands. There's a beautiful but simple silver ring on one of her fingers.)*

That ring? That's from me.

BRENDA. *No manches*, I *love* this ring!

IVONNE. I've got good taste.

BRENDA. *Mi mamá* said it was from one of her co-workers but I thought that was like code for like *los tres Reyes* or something.

IVONNE. Nope. Just me.

You'll wanna put that away, though. They'll take it from you if they see it.

BRENDA. *(Putting it in her pocket.)* Got it. Thanks.

What's your name again?

IVONNE. *Ivonne.*

BRENDA. *Mucho / gusto.*

IVONNE. Okay so here's everything you need to know. The older one over there? She's been here since we opened. She doesn't say much and she keeps to herself. If you need a little pick me up, she's got the good shit. Let me know and I can facilitate a little intro. And the one with the tight ass *chonga*? You don't wanna fuck with her. She's seen some shit and carries a *machete* in her purse. I know. *Esta bien loca.* It doesn't even fit. And the *flaquita* in the corner? Don't be fooled by that smile. She's got it out for almost everyone here. Rumor has it she's dating one of *los rebeldes* so it's best if you stay out of her way. But what do I know, it's only a rumor.

BRENDA. And Zaide? What's her deal?

IVONNE. Fuck Zaide.

BRENDA. Woah.

IVONNE. I'm only gonna say this once because I don't waste my breath on old irrelevant petty dumb ass bitches like her. Zaide's been here for forever. Not just this *maquila* but even the ones before they opened the border. She showed me the ropes when I first got here and I'm thankful for that, I am. But between you and me, and this stays between us girls, she's been looking for something or someone to blame for this whole thing. She's hysterical. She puts the blame on me because...the girls trust me more? I don't know. Maybe she's jealous. She used to be a pillar for the girls around here and she isn't anymore. *(Beat.)* Sucks to be left out.

BRENDA. Yeah. It does.

IVONNE. This place? It does things to you. If you've been here long enough you see these walls more than you see your own family.

> *(The sound of another buzzer is heard, signaling the end of the break. One by one, the women clock back in and return to work. They are at the same pace as they were before, if not faster. Breaths, grunts, and the wiping of sweat can be heard.)*

Andale, niña.

BRENDA. Wait...it's over? / Already?

IVONNE. It's over. Now come on, we gotta get back to –

BRENDA. But I didn't even get a chance to –

IVONNE. Boss doesn't like it when we stand around and chat, okay? We get two ten-minute breaks to pee, and we only have thirty minutes for lunch. Got it?

BRENDA. But what if I have to pee while I'm working?

IVONNE. Two breaks. Well, one now. Take sips of water – just for hydration.

BRENDA. And if I get thirsty?

IVONNE. I got a UTI once for holding it in too long. Water isn't worth it.

> *(**IVONNE** heads back to her work station.)*

(The women are working with rapid speed. The motion and choreography of their movement with the machines should feel like a dance, set in a fast-forward tempo.)

ALL.

MUY PRONTO EL PROLETARIADO CON LA RAZÓN
    VENCERÁ

MUY PRONTO EL PROLETARIADO CON LA RAZÓN
    VENCERÁ

LOS PRODUCTOS DEL TRABAJO DEL TRABAJADOR SERÁN

LOS PRODUCTOS DEL TRABAJO DEL TRABAJADOR SERÁN

SEMBRAREMOS EN LA LUCHA SEMILLAS DE LIBERTAD

SEMBRAREMOS EN LA LUCHA SEMILLAS DE LIBERTAD

LAS REGAREMOS DE IDEAS Y PRONTO GERMINARAN

LAS REGAREMOS DE IDEAS Y PRONTO GERMINARAN

TRABAJADORA ERES TU TRABAJADORA TAMBIÉN YO,
    TRABAJADORA ERES TU TRABAJADORA TAMBIÉN YO;

SI SEGUIMOS SEPARADAS NUNCA HABRÁ REVOLUCIÓN,

SI SEGUIMOS SEPARADAS NUNCA HABRÁ REVOLUCIÓN.

(A loud buzzer is heard, signaling the end of the day. The women slow their production to a stop and one by one clock out.)

BRENDA. Twelve hours a day, six days a week. How much do we get paid again?

IVONNE. *(Laughing.)* Enough to eat.

*(**BRENDA** presses the tips of her fingers against each other. They are raw.)*

BRENDA. I think I cut my fingers.

IVONNE. It's the thread. You'll grow calluses eventually.

*(She shows **BRENDA** her hands.)*

BRENDA. Ouch!

IVONNE. Try packing meat at the *Mercado Grande* in *Durango*. Ouch.

BRENDA. Where's *Durango*?

IVONNE. Far from here, *niña.*

BRENDA. What brought you to *Juárez*?

> (**IVONNE** *points outside a window where mountains can be seen.*)

IVONNE. There. That.

BRENDA. El Paso?

IVONNE. América. And *mi hermana.* She's the one who wanted to move here but...she couldn't stay.

BRENDA. My cousin wants me to move to the U.S., *pero mi mamá* says it's not all that great.

IVONNE. América is beautiful.

BRENDA. You've been to América?!

IVONNE. No. But I can imagine.

BRENDA. Well what are you waiting for? You should go.

> (*Beat.*)

IVONNE. *Mi novio Raúl.* He wants to take me there.

BRENDA. *Mi mamá* says men only want one thing.

IVONNE. (*Laughing.*) Do you listen to everything Yolanda tells you?

BRENDA. Not everything. She told me not to quit school, that she'd find a way to get the money we needed, but I quit anyway.

IVONNE. I had to work three jobs when I first moved here to get by. It wasn't easy because my sister liked going out and she...yeah. Everything comes at cost.

(There is small discreet chatter among the women as they clump together, forming a small congregation. Before leaving the factory, they link arms and march slowly downstage center to speak to the maquila owner. **BRENDA** *and* **IVONNE** *stand aside.)*

BRENDA. What's going on?

IVONNE. Sh, *niña, no.*

ZAIDE. *(Out to the audience.) Disciple Señor.* All we are asking...is for *la ruta* to drop us off a little closer to our houses. Just for those of us working the night shift, that's it.

> *(Beat.)*

Some of us have to walk at least five blocks from the bus stop and –

> *(Beat.)*

I know these streets are owned by rival gangs, but a little closer, just at night, that's –

> *(Beat.)*

Yes but sometimes I run so fast in that one block I almost run into my door. And I'm not the only one, it's all of us.

> *(Beat. Quiet danger.)*

My name? *Porque?*

> *(Beat. Hesitant.)*

Zaide.

> *(Beat. This is hard.)*

Zaide Florencia de la O.

(Defeated.) Si. Si. Okay. Gracias.

(She starts to walk out, but then –.)

Mm? Oh.

Yeah. See you tomorrow.

(The women leave the maquiladora and get on la ruta, the bus that takes them to and from the maquilas. Exhausted. It's dark out. Too dark.)

(As they ride the bus, some women have headphones plugged into old Walkman cassette players, others carry rosaries, all of them sing.)

(ZAIDE slowly starts to fall sleep. One by one, the other women exit the bus until ZAIDE is left alone.)

ALL (EXCEPT ZAIDE).
TRABAJADORA ERES TÚ TRABAJADORA TAMBIÉN YO,
   TRABAJADORA ERES TÚ TRABAJADORA TAMBIÉN YO;
SI SEGUIMOS SEPARADAS NUNCA HABRÁ REVOLUCIÓN,
SI SEGUIMOS SEPARADAS NUNCA HABRÁ REVOLUCIÓN
   TRABAJADORA ERES TÚ TRABAJADORA TAMBIÉN YO,
   TRABAJADORA ERES TÚ TRABAJADORA TAMBIÉN YO;
SI SEGUIMOS SEPARADAS NUNCA HABRÁ REVOLUCIÓN,
SI SEGUIMOS SEPARADAS NUNCA HABRÁ REVOLUCIÓN

(The bus comes to an abrupt stop and ZAIDE is jostled awake. She does not recognize her location. She makes her way towards the front of the bus.)

ZAIDE. *Señor,* I think I fell asleep and missed my stop. Where are we?

(A moment. No response.)

Señor?

(Lights shift.)

Three
Green Enchiladas and a Mother's Broken Heart

(Projections: **FRIDAY JULY 10, 1998. THREE DAYS AFTER BRENDA'S DISAPPEARANCE.***)*

(Yolanda's small, humble, adobe home in Ciudad Juárez.)

(The floor is made of concrete and large blankets pinned to the ceiling with old wooden clothespins to separate each room. Folded laundry is stacked neatly on an ironing board. There's no one inside the house, but **YOLANDA** *might be seen taking more clothes down from the clothes line outside in the backyard.)*

(A moment.)

(Then, like a whirlwind, **IVONNE** *bursts through the front door, slamming it shut behind her, catching her breath as if she'd been running for miles. Her clothes are ripped and dirty, with blood stains on her knees and elbows. Her hair is disheveled and her makeup is smeared. Something terrible has just happened to her.)*

*(***YOLANDA** *quickly enters the room, carrying clean laundry from outside.)*

YOLANDA.   Brenda? *(Beat.)* Ivonne, / *(1)* oh my god, Ivonne! What the...what happened to you, is that blood? *(Beat.)* Brenda! Where is she. Where's my Brendita, is she outside?

*(***YOLANDA** *throws the door open and runs outside.)*

Brenda!

> *(Nothing.)*

Brendita?

> *(Nothing.)*

> **(YOLANDA** *disappears as she searches the back and sides of her house for Brenda.)*

> *(A moment. Then.)*

> *(Offstage.)*

BRENDA!!!!

IVONNE. *(Derailing.) (1)* Yolanda I I I I... I'm fine, it's just a little... *FUCK!* It fucking *HURTS, ay ay ay ay ay ay ay ay* ow ow ow ow ow ow ow ow I can't breathe, Lord *por favor,* I can't breathe, I can't breathe...

> **(IVONNE** *falls into herself completely.)*

> **(YOLANDA** *rushes back inside the house, slamming the door behind her.)*

YOLANDA. I thought you left together. That's why she's been gone, because...you left together.

IVONNE. Yolanda, please –

YOLANDA. So she's really...

She's...gone?

> **(YOLANDA** *has gone somewhere else. She bites her nails. She loses her daughter all over again. She doesn't cry, but she starts to fall into herself.)*

IVONNE. Yoli...

Yolanda.

Yoli.

Yolanda.

Yolanda.

Yolanda.

Yolanda.

Yolanda.

Yoli.

Yoli please.

Yoli please just –

Look at me Yolanda. I'm here.

I'm here.

I'm here.

> *(Beat. A moment.)*

YOLANDA. *(Snapping out of it.)* You're here.

> *(Beat.)*

> *(Something has changed.)*

You know you can't just *disappear* like that Ivonne, you *know* that.

> *(She sees a twig in* **IVONNE***'s hair. Pulls it out and tosses it aside.)*

There. That's better. *Ay que bonita,* I love that blouse. Is that Brenda's?

> *(Beat.)*

IVONNE. *(Trying to keep it together.)* Mhmm.

> *(A moment.)*

YOLANDA. You know the police said we gotta wait three days before they'll look for her. That's what they said, three days. But that's okay, because Brenda will come back.

She's coming back.

She is.

(A moment.)

What are you doing standing there like that Ivonne, sit. Please, please sit. I'm making green enchiladas. They're almost ready, have some. I made way too much.

(Beat.)

(Beat.)

(Beat.)

(Beat.)

IVONNE. Okay.

(IVONNE sits at the table, on the edge of her seat. There's a young girl's blouse sitting between them on the table. Brenda's blouse. IVONNE stares at it. YOLANDA stares at IVONNE.)

(A moment. YOLANDA grabs the top and puts it away.)

YOLANDA. I'll just leave these over here and she can do with them whatever she wants when she gets back, no fuss, no mess.

(Beat.)

What's that smell is that...

(She smells. A moment.)

IVONNE. Um.

>   (**IVONNE** *presses her knees together.*)

>   (**YOLANDA** *goes to one of her cajones and pulls out some incense or a candle. Lights it and sets it on the table. She sits down beside her.*)

I...

Tripped on my way over here.

and...mud...yeah.

>   (*In a quickness, a car stops close by playing some kind of corrido, maybe it's a narco corrido; its headlights painfully visible through Yolanda's lack of blinds.*)

>   (**IVONNE***'s head quickly turns towards it. Her breathing intensifies. The sound of the motor still running, headlights pressing on.*)

>   (**IVONNE** *ducks immediately.*)

Can you see the color of that van, the one parked outside?

>   (**YOLANDA** *takes a step towards the window.*)

Not too close.

YOLANDA. (*Taking another step.*) What, / why?

IVONNE. I said not too close!

YOLANDA. You're scaring me.

>   (*Beat.*)

>   (*A moment.*)

>   (*Then.*)

IVONNE. From where you're standing...can you see the color of the van...the one parked outside...

> *(Squinting.)*

YOLANDA. Um...

> *(**YOLANDA** takes one more step towards the window and looks through it.)*

It's blue.

> *(And just like that, the car drives off.)*

> *(Beat.)*

> *(Beat.)*

> *(Beat.)*

> *(Beat.)*

IVONNE. *(Quiet; near tears.)* I'm leaving Juárez.

YOLANDA. What?

IVONNE. First thing tomorrow morning. I'm meeting my cousins in *El Porvenir* / and –

YOLANDA. Wait wait wait wait slow down. You're *leaving*?

IVONNE. Come with me.

YOLANDA. *Qué?*

IVONNE. Come with me. Let's get out of here, go away, go far away from all this and never look back, just the two of us, don't you want / that?

YOLANDA. I I I I can't just go, Brenda's gonna walk through that door any minute now and I I I –

IVONNE. She's not coming back, Yolanda!

> *(Beat. **IVONNE** covers her mouth.)*

YOLANDA. You do know something.

IVONNE. That's not what I. You know what I.

YOLANDA. Some people said they saw you with her in *El Centro*. / Is that true?

IVONNE. I don't... No.

YOLANDA. Because you always ride the bus with her –

IVONNE. I do.

YOLANDA. But not that night?

IVONNE. I already said no –

YOLANDA. Okay then so *why* weren't you with her?

IVONNE. I don't know.

YOLANDA. You were supposed to look out for her.

IVONNE. I know I was.

YOLANDA. *So why weren't you with her?!*

IVONNE. I DON'T KNOW!!!

YOLANDA. Okay then GET OUT. Get out of my house! Get out of her clothes, just GET OUT!

>   (**YOLANDA** *grabs a pile of laundry, and throws them at* **IVONNE**.)

(*Quiet.*) Whatever it is... I don't want to be anywhere near it. So get out.

>   (**IVONNE** *stares at* **YOLANDA** *in complete disbelief.*)

>   (*Beat.*)

>   (*Beat.*)

>   (*Beat.*)

>   (*Beat.*)

*(And just like that, **IVONNE** is gone.)*

(A moment.)

*(Then, **YOLANDA** rushes over to the thrown laundry on the floor. Fuck. They're dirty.)*

(To herself.) No, no, no, no, no, no, no...

(She dusts dirt off of them and begins folding them neatly, over and over again. For every crease that isn't crisp she tries again with immense precision. As she folds, she sings to calm herself down. A new ritual forming right before our very eyes.)

[III. "CIELITO LINDO"]

DE LA SIERRA MORENA,
CIELITO LINDO, VIENEN BAJANDO,
UN PAR DE OJITOS NEGROS,
CIELITO LINDO, DE CONTRABANDO.

AY, AY, AY, AY
CANTA Y NO LLORES
PORQUE CANTANDO SE ALEGRAN
CIELITO LINDO, LOS CORAZONES

(She folds...)

(And folds...)

(And folds...)

(Lights shift.)

Four
Salsa Verde and Fires in the Sky

(Projections: **SATURDAY, JULY 4, 1998. THREE DAYS BEFORE BRENDA'S DISAPPEARANCE.***)*

(Yolanda's small, humble, adobe home in Ciudad Juárez.)

(The living room is covered in dirty, unkept laundry. Stacks of jeans fall off an ironing board.)

*(****BRENDA*** *is still in her maquila uniform. She tosses clothes everywhere. She looks hard for something.)*

BRENDA. Come onnnnnn. It's gotta be here somewhere...

*(****MARISELA*** *enters carrying stacks of corner store trash bags tied and full to the brim with several kinds of tamales. They are heavy.)*

(She yells out into the other room as she enters:)

MARISELA. *(Yelling; towards the kitchen.)* Oye Yolanda, don't forget the *salsa verde*! You know how Yesenia gets if we fuck up her order, and we've got a *lot* of *tamales* in here.

(Seeing **BRENDA.***)*

Brendita! Gracias a Dios, you're home early! *Oye,* can you take these *por favor*? My arms aren't what they used to be.

*(****BRENDA*** *rushes over, grabs the tamales and puts them down on the table.)*

Ay, there you go. *Hijole!* Carrying these up and down the house makes my heart race!

> (**BRENDA**, *distracted, keeps looking. Mildly entertaining* **MARISELA** *as she talks.*)

BRENDA. Oh yeah? That sucks.

MARISELA. You know, I hated working at the *maquila,* but it sure beat the hell out of making and selling *pinche tamales* like it's Christmas Eve.

BRENDA. Yeah, yeah.

MARISELA. I never thought *tu Amá* and I would get *fired.* Fewer hours, sure, but *fired*?

BRENDA. *Que cool.*

MARISELA. But at least we have our *tamales.*

BRENDA. Mhmm.

MARISELA. We could start a little *tamal* shop! We could call it *Yoli y Maris.* OR, *Mari y Yolis,* which one sounds better?

BRENDA. Yes.

> *(Beat.)*

> (**MARISELA** *notices* **BRENDA** *isn't really listening to her.*)

MARISELA. We already have an order for *La Llorona tambíen.* She's a real treat. You know. With all her crying.

BRENDA. That's nice.

> *(Beat.)*

> (**MARISELA** *grabs her chancla and throws it at* **BRENDA.** *It hits her hard on the ass.*)

(**BRENDA** *looks up from her pile of mess.*)

Hey!

MARISELA. What the hell's your problem, huh? You can't respect your elders when they're talking to you?

BRENDA. Sorry, Mari. Ivonne invited me to pop fireworks with her and her friends by the desert and –

MARISELA. Fireworks? What fireworks, for what?

BRENDA. For the fourth.

(*A moment.*)

Of July…?

(*A moment.*)

Independence day?

MARISELA. Independence for who? I don't see no independence.

BRENDA. I'm trying to find this blouse I haven't worn in like a million years, and Ivonne's waiting for me outside and I'm *stressed out* right now!!!

MARISELA. And Yolanda's okay with this?

(*Beat.*)

BRENDA. Uh huh.

MARISELA. Really?

BRENDA. Mhmm. I talked to her this morning.

MARISELA. Hm.

(*A moment.*)

(*Yelling.*) YOLA / NDA!

BRENDA. Okay, okay I haven't actually asked her yet, *sheesh*!

MARISELA. You know the rules. If you want to hang out with Ivonne, you need to hang out with her at the house.

BRENDA. All my friends get to go out, why can't I?

MARISELA. If your friends jump off a cliff, would you?

BRENDA. / No.

MARISELA. No. That's right. So you listen to *tu mamá* and you go tell Itzel / that if she wants to hang out with her bestie *Brendita* that she can do so here, at the house, while Yolanda is home. *Entiendes?*

BRENDA. Ivonne.

(Disappointed, annoyed.) Si.

MARISELA. *Mierdas estúpidas. Pinches gringos pendejos* with those fireworks, shooting those stupid candlesticks at each other, *uy!*

(Beat.)

You don't want *tu Amá* up all hours of the day and night worried about you, *euh?* About where you are, what you're doing, or worse?

BRENDA. Of course not.

MARISELA. But you girls don't *think,* you never *think.* You think because you're a teenager that you're invincible, like you've got it all figured out, well I'm sorry to be a bubble blaster or however you say it but you're not, okay, you're not.

BRENDA. Okay. I got it. I'm sorry.

MARISELA. It's for your own good, *Brendita.*

BRENDA. I know.

MARISELA. Good.

(Beat. A moment.)

BRENDA. I'm...sorry about Rubí, Mari. I've been meaning to stop by, but with work and / stuff...

MARISELA. *No, no, si, si.*

Thank you.

BRENDA. Any updates?

MARISELA. Nope. Six months is a long time.

BRENDA. *Claro.*

MARISELA. But. She'll turn up soon enough. I'm sure of it. I will find her. I'm determined.

BRENDA. *Claro.*

MARISELA. *Claro.*

> (**MARISELA** *smiles weakly.*)
>
> (*A moment.*)

BRENDA. I'm gonna go tell Ivonne I can't go.

MARISELA. Okay. *Pero apúrate,* the sun's setting.

> (**BRENDA** *smiles weakly and leaves.*)
>
> (*A moment.* **MARISELA** *is lost in her thoughts.*)
>
> (*Then.*)
>
> (**YOLANDA** *enters just as* **BRENDA** *closes the door behind her. Her hands are covered in fresh masa harina. She wipes her hands on her jeans as she enters.*)

YOLANDA. Alright, that should be the last of them. Got the last dozen steaming as we speak. Was that Brenda? She's home early.

MARISELA. *(Shady-like.)* Mhmm.

YOLANDA. What's that about?

MARISELA. I don't like that girl she's been hanging out with. Ile.

YOLANDA. *Ivonne.* You know who she is, Mari.

MARISELA. I don't trust her. She's always dressing *bien naca* with the hoops and the *pinche* crop tops like she's on *Muchachitas.*

YOLANDA. Mari, be nice.

MARISELA. Even at the *maquilas* she would dress like that.

(*Beat.*)

You trust her?

YOLANDA. I do. She acts like she's hard, but really she's just a kid, just like *Brendita,* just like we were when we were in our twenties. Remember that?

MARISELA. No.

YOLANDA. Brendita likes her and I trust Brenda.

(**YOLANDA**'s *phone rings from the other room.*)

Ay, that's probably Yesenia. How many *salsa verdes* did she order?

MARISELA. I don't know.

YOLANDA. You didn't write it down?

MARISELA. No.

(*Beat.*)

YOLANDA. We're not gonna make good business if you don't write the orders down.

MARISELA. Why didn't *you* write it down?

(*The phone keeps ringing.*)

Pues aren't you gonna answer it?

(As she storms off.)

YOLANDA. *(Under her breath.)* *Chinga tu madre.* I have to do *everything* myself around here, / *chingado...*

MARISELA. You live here!

> *(As* **YOLANDA** *makes her way to the kitchen, the sound of girls laughing just outside the front entrance can be heard.)*

Oh great.

> *(***IVONNE** *and* **BRENDA** *come in.)*

Ilana! Como estas?

IVONNE. Ivonne.

MARISELA. *Ay, si, si, si. Perdoname.* Old age.

IVONNE. How are you, Mari? It's been forever.

BRENDA. *(To* **IVONNE.***)* My room's / over here.

MARISELA. How's the *maquila*?

IVONNE. Oh, you know.

MARISELA. *(A la chisme; to* **IVONNE.***)* What's the latest?

IVONNE. *(To* **MARI.***)* *Blancita* is pregnant.

MARISELA. *(To* **IVONNE.***)* *No!*

BRENDA. Or not, we can hang out here.

IVONNE. I had to hide her machete.

MARISELA. *(To* **IVONNE.***)* *A la chingada!*

BRENDA. *Ay* I have to pee so bad!

> *(***BRENDA** *rushes over to the bathroom, which is on the other side of pinned blankets, on the opposite side of the kitchen.)*

> *(A moment.)*

IVONNE. *(To* MARI.*)* Where's Yolanda?

MARISELA. *Tiene* phone call.

IVONNE. Who?

MARISELA. Yesenia.

IVONNE. Ew.

> *(Beat.)*
>
> *(Beat.)*
>
> *(Beat.)*
>
> *(Beat.)*

Your hair looks great, Mari.

MARISELA. Thanks...

IVONNE. I got mine done yesterday.

MARISELA. Huh.

> *(Beat.)*
>
> *(Beat.)*
>
> *(Beat.)*
>
> *(Beat.)*
>
> (**BRENDA** *emerges from the bathroom.)*

BRENDA. So are we doing this or what?

IVONNE. Yes, please.

MARISELA. What are you girls up to?

BRENDA. We're gonna watch the fireworks from outside.

MARISELA. Oh. Can I come?

IVONNE. / Sure.

BRENDA. N / o.

IVONNE. No.

MARISELA. But not for too long, okay? I gotta print new fliers to hand out. I think I... I think I'm ready to look for her myself.

>   *(Beat. No one says anything.)*

>   *(The fireworks start popping from a distance.)*

IVONNE. Well, what are we waiting for?

>   *(More fireworks pop.)*

BRENDA. Last one out gets *chorrito*!

MARISELA. *(Laughing.) Cochina!*

>   *(They all rush outside, the fireworks popping in the desert behind them, dancing like little fires in the night sky. A brief moment of peace.)*

>   *(They pop and pop and pop.)*

>   *(Lights shift.)*

Five
Sisters by Water

(Projections: **MONDAY, AUGUST 17, 1998. ONE MONTH AND TEN DAYS AFTER BRENDA'S DISAPPEARANCE.***)*

(Yolanda's same small, humble, adobe home in Ciudad Juárez.)

(The living room is covered in clean laundry. Yolanda's clothes are covered in stains from masa harina from making batches of tamales.)

*(***YOLANDA*** folds the same series of clean laundry over and over again while occasionally looking out the window for someone. She hums a familiar tune as she does this, singing to herself casually to pass the time.)*

[IV. "CIELITO LINDO – REVISITED"]

YOLANDA.

DE LA SIERRA MORENA,
CIELITO LINDO, VIENEN BAJANDO,
UN PAR DE OJITOS NEGROS,
CIELITO LINDO, DE CONTRABANDO.
AY, AY, AY, AY
CANTA Y NO –

> *(A loud knock at the door.* **YOLANDA** *rises from her chair and peeks through the window to see who is outside. She sees who it is and immediately stops singing. Another knock.* **YOLANDA** *is frozen. Silent.)*

MARISELA. Yoli.

(Another knock. Silence.)

Yolanda.

(Incessant knocking. Still nothing.)

I know you're in there, I heard you singing.

> *(Beat.* **YOLANDA** *takes in a deep breath and brushes the hair out of her face with her fingers. She unlocks and opens the door.)*

YOLANDA. Marisela. Hey.

MARISELA. Hey? All you can say to me is...hey?

YOLANDA. Please. Please come in.

MARISELA. I'm fine right here.

> *(Silence.)*

> *(Beat.)*

> *(Beat.)*

> *(Beat.)*

> *(Beat.)*

(Holding a large tupperware.) I was putting some things away and found this. It's not mine so I figured it's yours. I don't really talk to anyone else.

YOLANDA. We made *sopa* for Rubí when she got pneumonia last year. I told Brenda not to go over 'cause I knew she'd get sick too but she never listens.

> *(A moment.)*

I know the girls weren't close or anything, but... I just wanted them to get along, you know? Just like us.

MARISELA. Yeah, just like us.

(Beat.)

(A moment.)

Her burial was last week. I kept looking around for you but you never came. Did you not get my message?

YOLANDA. I –

> *(**MARISELA** pulls out a crumpled piece of paper from her pocket.)*

MARISELA. I brought her *recuerdo*. Has the prayer I wrote for her on the back and everything.

> *(Beat.)*

You were right...it wasn't José.

YOLANDA. I didn't want to be right, Mari.

MARISELA. But you were.

> *(A moment.)*

The boyfriend...

He's uh...with *Los Zetas*...so...

> *(Beat.)*

> *(**YOLANDA** reaches for **MARISELA**.)*

(Tender.) Don't. Don't touch me. Don't.

> *(After a moment, **MARISELA** is overcome with emotion and grief and falls into herself. It starts off small but avalanches until she loses it completely. **YOLANDA** places a hand on her shoulder, and then slowly pulls her into a full embrace. She leads her into the house and sits her down on the couch.)*

YOLANDA. Sh. Shhhh. It's okay, Mari, it's okay.

MARISELA. I miss her so much. Every day is harder than the last. I keep telling myself this isn't real, that I'm in a dream and that someday I'll wake up. But I don't.

YOLANDA. *Ay Marisela...*

MARISELA. It hurts to talk. It hurts to breathe. Her memory follows me everywhere and I don't know what to do with it. I keep thinking back to the last time I saw her. I still remember her yellow blouse, the mole on her neck, the dimple on her cheek. She smiled. And she said, "I'll see you soon, *mamá*."

You never notice the little things until they're not there anymore.

YOLANDA. It's the little things that keep them alive.

MARISELA. But she's not alive...how can I keep her alive... when she's not?

> *(A moment.* **YOLANDA** *cannot answer this.)*

> *(Beat.)*

When my little girl went missing, I spent months. Months. Looking for her *everywhere*.

YOLANDA. We looked together.

MARISELA. And do you have any idea what they gave me instead of my beautiful girl?

> *(A moment.* **YOLANDA** *shakes her head.)*

A pile of sand and a bag of bones. Pieces of her chopped up and left in the dumpster.

YOLANDA. *Ay, qué bárbaro.*

MARISELA. And did you hear what happened to *him*? After his confession, at the court house.

> *(***YOLANDA** *shakes her head.)*

Nothing.

They let him go.

Just like that, just...let him go.

YOLANDA. Unbelievable.

MARISELA. Is it?

(*Beat.*)

I met a bunch of women at her burial? *Mujeres* whose daughters are still missing. They've been helpful. Depressing, but helpful.

YOLANDA. The ones who sing by the crosses...?

MARISELA. *Si.*

YOLANDA. *Ay* Marisela...are you sure it's safe being around them right now? You've seen them at *El Centro* with all those protests and demonstrations? You really want to be caught up in all that?

MARISELA. Yes. No. I don't know.

(*A moment.*)

They uh...they invited me to one of their weekly meetings. At *Casa Amiga*?

(*Beat.*)

I think I might check it out.

YOLANDA. I don't know Marisela...

MARISELA. One meeting. Just to see, you know?

I might hate it.

But it also might help.

I was hoping, maybe...you'd wanna come with me?

YOLANDA. Oh Mari, I don't know about all that...

MARISELA. I can't walk in there alone.

YOLANDA. Yes you can, you're braver than you think.

MARISELA. Am I?

YOLANDA. Of course you are, *bebita.* You are one of the bravest people I know. It just...doesn't feel right for me to be there.

>   *(Beat.)*

MARISELA. I thought this was something we could do together.

YOLANDA. Together? Like going to the park?

MARISELA. I think this meeting would be good for us.

YOLANDA. Good for us or good for you?

MARISELA. Good for both of us.

YOLANDA. Are you hearing yourself?

>   *Están locas.*

MARISELA. You're more alike than you think.

YOLANDA. I'm nothing like them.

MARISELA. A lot of them work at the *maquila.*

YOLANDA. That doesn't mean I'm anything like them.

MARISELA. A lot of them have been getting phone calls, too.

>   *(Beat.)*

YOLANDA. You told them about me?

MARISELA. No, of course not.

YOLANDA. 'Cause that's not your business to tell.

MARISELA. I know that, Yolanda.

YOLANDA. Three years. That's what they said. Three / years.

MARISELA. They're lying to you, / Yoli.

YOLANDA. You don't know that.

MARISELA. That's what these men do. They lie. They call and tell us that they have our daughters and that when they're done using them for – do you know what they use them for? They use them as sex slaves. / Trafficking.

YOLANDA. Stop it!

MARISELA. Do you really believe them when they say they're gonna return her to you, Yoli?

YOLANDA. Yes.

MARISELA. Well I don't. And even if they did, she wouldn't be the same. Brenda would be / changed forever.

YOLANDA. Did you get any phone calls?

MARISELA. No.

YOLANDA. So maybe it was different for you than it is for me. Ever think about that?

    (Beat.)

Did you know who Rubí was hanging out with? At any moment, at any time?

MARISELA. Not all the time, no –

YOLANDA. Because that's what they're saying. On the news? That Rubí and these girls are at the *cantinas* in *El Centro,* hanging around the wrong kind of guys.

MARISELA. So Brenda was hanging around the wrong kind of guys?

YOLANDA. She's not hanging around *Los Zetas,* if that's what you're saying.

MARISELA. But you think Rubí was.

YOLANDA. Wasn't she?

MARISELA. I *know* she wasn't.

YOLANDA. I don't want to talk about this anymore, Marisela.

MARISELA. Oh, we're just getting started.

YOLANDA. I said I'm done talking about this.

MARISELA. That won't make it go away.

YOLANDA. I said I'M / DONE.

MARISELA. I HELD MY BABY'S *TEETH* IN MY *HANDS*, YOLANDA!

YOLANDA. AND I HAVEN'T! And I have no choice but to believe that Brenda is still out there, okay, I don't.

> *(A moment.)*

> *(Beat.)*

I'm really, really, *really* sorry about Rubí, Marisela. I am. And I'm sorry I wasn't there when you needed me. But what did you want me to do? I couldn't just stand there and watch you bury yourself with her. I just... I couldn't.

> *(Beat.)*

> *(Beat.)*

> *(Beat.)*

> *(Beat.)*

MARISELA. You're upset.

YOLANDA. I'm not / upset.

MARISELA. *I* think you're upset. That's the only thing I can say to keep myself from smacking you for talking to me like that. You're upset.

> *(A moment.)*

(The two of them just stand there facing each other. A stand-off.)

*(***YOLANDA*** motions to her front door.)*

YOLANDA. Thank you for stopping by.

(Beat.)

(Beat.)

(Beat.)

(Beat.)

*(***MARISELA*** grabs her purse and slowly heads towards the door. Stops herself.)*

MARISELA. *Que Dios te bendiga.*

*(***MARISELA*** leaves, slamming the door behind her. ***YOLANDA*** walks over to her pile of laundry. She takes a pair of jeans, smells them, unfolds and begins folding them all over again.)*

(Lights shift.)

Six
Bathroom Breaks and Broken Mirrors

(Projections: **THURSDAY, JULY 2, 1998. FIVE DAYS BEFORE BRENDA'S DISAPPEARANCE.***)*

(A washroom inside the maquiladora.)

*(***IVONNE** *is on the phone.)*

IVONNE. No no no no no no we had a deal, I thought we had a deal...it's been three years, you told me after three years...of course not, do you think I'm an idiot? ... I'm not doing that, I'm not... Because... I know... I said I know... Give me a few weeks, just a few weeks, then I –

> *(A shift. Someone else is on the phone now.)*

Erika?

Sh sh sh sh *no llores chiquita* I'm here I'm right here. I will be there soon, okay? Be strong okay? I love you so so so much. You know that right? ... Okay. Okay I will see you soon. *Te quiero mucho hermana* –

> *(The person on the other line has hung up the phone.* **IVONNE** *closes her flip phone, throws it in her clutch. She unleashes the most guttural scream. One from the pit of the earth.)*
>
> *(She paces a bit before stopping to take a look in the mirror.)*
>
> *(After a moment, she takes off her shoe and hits the mirror again and again and again until it breaks. Somewhere in the midst of this,* **BRENDA** *enters.)*

BRENDA. Ivonne?

IVONNE. *Ay chinga tu puta madre!* What the fuck are you doing, / standing there all scary and shit fuck. Almost gave me a heart attack.

BRENDA. Sorry, sorry, sorry!

I needed to pee, that's all.

(A moment.)

Was that you screaming, are you okay?

(Beat.)

IVONNE. The mirror's broken.

BRENDA. I can see that.

IVONNE. You know they never wash these? Fuckers. I can never see my own *pinche* face.

BRENDA. I guess I would have broken it too.

IVONNE. I didn't break it.

BRENDA. Yes you did.

IVONNE. No I didn't.

BRENDA. I saw you.

IVONNE. You didn't see anything.

BRENDA. I literally saw you / grab your shoe and –

IVONNE. You didn't see anything.

In fact, you were never here.

You don't exist. You are nothing.

Not even a breath in a whisper.

Got it?

BRENDA. Got it.

(The two stand there for a bit.)

(**BRENDA** *picks up shards of broken mirror and throws them in the trash. A moment.*)

IVONNE. Come here, *chiquita*.

BRENDA. You don't have to do that.

IVONNE. I wanna get a good look at you, come here.

(**BRENDA** *gets close.*)

(**IVONNE** *holds her face in her hands.*)

What foundation do you use?

BRENDA. Huh?

IVONNE. Foundation. What brand do you use?

BRENDA. Oh... I'm not allowed to wear makeup till I turn eighteen.

IVONNE. God, Yolanda's intense.

BRENDA. I know.

IVONNE. Well. She's gonna have to get over it.

(**IVONNE** *opens her clutch and pulls out a tube of mascara.*)

A little mascara never hurt anyone.

(*She applies to* **BRENDA**'s *eyes.*)

Blink.

Blink.

Not all the way! Watch the bottom, it stains.

There. A true beauty. Here. You keep it.

(*She hands the tube to* **BRENDA**.)

It's waterproof.

BRENDA. Thank you.

IVONNE. You have great skin, you know. Mine used to look like that. But one day I woke up and saw the world's troubles finally catch up with me. And they all decided to rest on my face.

BRENDA. You have amazing skin.

IVONNE. I have amazing foundation. Hides my stress lines.

BRENDA. Hides more than that.

  (Beat.)

IVONNE. If you've got something to say, say it to my face.

BRENDA. I'm not trying to fight you Ivonne.

IVONNE. Of course you're not. Walking around this place all nice and sweet when like it or not? You're just like the rest of us.

BRENDA. That's where you're wrong. I don't keep secrets from my friends.

IVONNE. That's because you *have* no friend, Brenda.

  (Beat. A moment.)

I'm sorry, that was. That was mean.

BRENDA. Yeah. It was.

IVONNE. You really think I keep things from you?

BRENDA. We hang out all the time and you say so much about everybody else but every time I ask about you, you change the subject.

IVONNE. I'm not that interesting.

BRENDA. Yes you are.

IVONNE. You don't know what interesting is.

BRENDA. There you go, doing it again. Talking to me like I'm a *pinche idiota,* well I'm not. What's going on? You've been acting strange all day. Is it Raúl? Is he being weird again?

(*A moment.*)

IVONNE. Something like that.

BRENDA. Why does he keep doing this? You gotta let that one go, you're so much better than that.

(*Beat.*)

IVONNE. You look just like her.

BRENDA. Who?

IVONNE. Erika.

BRENDA. You think so?

IVONNE. Yes. It's your eyes. They're soft, have a little haze around them. But they're also piercing, like... inescapable. Just like hers.

BRENDA. Is that a good thing?

IVONNE. Oh yeah.

BRENDA. You miss her?

IVONNE. She's my sister.

BRENDA. Well... Why don't you pay her a visit? She's back in *Durango, no*?

(*Beat.*)

IVONNE. Yeah.

BRENDA. Maybe we could go together. It'll be fun! Like a little road trip or something!

IVONNE. Sure. I'd like that.

BRENDA. *Ya ves?* You *can* be a nice person.

(They laugh.)

IVONNE. *Callate gacha!*

BRENDA. You know I'm just messing with you.

IVONNE. I know, I know.

(A moment.)

I love you, *Brendita.*

BRENDA. Okay? Random. I love you too, Ivonne.

IVONNE. Should probably get back to work. Break's almost up.

BRENDA. Oh shoot I still gotta pee.

(BRENDA goes into one of the stalls and pees. Sigh of relief.)

(IVONNE quietly leaves.)

I don't know if I'm cut out for this, Ivonne. I have a small bladder and I feel like I'm gonna explode like every day. I finally started putting some money away so that's good. Hopefully I'll save up enough by Christmas to get *mi mamá* something real nice. She'd like that, no?

(Toilet flush. She comes out. IVONNE is nowhere in sight.)

Ivonne?

(BRENDA notices she's alone.)

Great.

(She washes her hands.)

(Dries them on her jeans (they're out of paper towels).)

(She notices **IVONNE** *left her clutch on the counter.)*

Oh.

(She looks around before opening it to see what's inside.)

(She pulls out a tube of lipstick. Puts some on as best she can without a mirror.)

(A phone starts ringing from inside Ivonne's clutch.)

(It's her cell phone.)

(BRENDA *looks around. Grabs it. After a moment, she answers.)*

Hello?

(The sound of men breathing.)

...hello?

(Lights shift.)

Seven
Siete Soles

(Projections: **WEDNESDAY AUGUST 23, 2000. TWO YEARS AND FORTY-SEVEN DAYS AFTER BRENDA'S DISAPPEARANCE.***)*

(10:17 a.m.)

(The sun blazes fiercely on Campo Algodonero – a cotton field in the outskirts of Ciudad Juárez, México. The sand is still and tranquil. A small wind blows and for a moment, everything is still.)

(Several pink crosses are placed firmly within the desert sand and are bare. There are names written on these crosses, but they are now faded and illegible. They have been there for many, many years.)

*(***IVONNE*** is seen kneeling by these crosses. She wears a faded and ripped blouse. Her jeans are dirty and have several holes in them. Her hair is disheveled and is tangled with dirt and mud. She kneels, barefoot, by loose sand. It's extraordinarily hot. She is unfazed by this.)*

(She holds a deep red rosario in her hand, and she is praying.)

(A moment.)

(The sound of the wind against the hot, coarse desert sand. We sit in this for awhile.)

(Then.)

(The wind against the desert sand turns into a beat of some kind. The sound of percussion that can only be heard in the depths of the desert. A sound both painfully unreal, and hauntingly familiar all at once.)

(Is it music? Is it the sun? Is it the wind? Perhaps it is neither. Perhaps it is all of the above.)

(All the same, **IVONNE** *prays. The sounds of the desert turn into song.* **IVONNE** *closes her eyes and is swallowed by it. The voice she hears sounds a lot like* **DESAMAYA**.)

(The sun burns like fire on hands.)

[V. "SIETE SOLES"]

DESAMAYA. *(Joined by everyone; the women of Juárez, cardenche style.)*

VENGO DEL POZO PROFUNDO
DEL FIN DEL MUNDO
TRAIGO CONMIGO EL POLVO
DE LOS CAMINOS
YA NO ME QUEDA NADA
TODO LO SÉ PERDIDO
DICEN QUE ALLÁ EN EL NORTE ESTÁ MI DESTINO.

> *(**IVONNE** opens her eyes. She's somewhere else. She joins in.)*

ME ENCANDILAN LOS RAYOS
DE SIETE SOLES
ME ENCEGUESE LA SAL
DEL LLANTO VERTIDO
YA NADA ME DE TIENE
YA ME VESTÍ DE OLVIDO
SUPE QUE ALLÁ EN EL NORTE ESTÁ MI DESTINO.

SÓLO SECÓ MIS LÁGRIMAS EL DESIERTO
SÓLO MATÓ MIS SUEÑOS LA OSCURIDAD
SÓLO SEGUÍ EL DESTELLO DE UN ESPEJISMO
BAJO LOS SIETE SOLES
CAÍ AL ABISMO.

> *(The drum of the desert beats furiously.)*

> *(The sound of the wind dances wildly.)*

> *(Then, as if every woman in Juárez were right there with her, every name on a cross, every name on every balcony, on every street, on every bus, on every sidewalk.)*

ALL.
SÓLO SECÓ MIS LÁGRIMAS EL DESIERTO
SÓLO MATÓ MIS SUEÑOS LA OSCURIDAD
SÓLO SEGUÍ EL DESTELLO DE UN ESPEJISMO

DESAMAYA.
BAJO LOS SIETE SOLES
CAÍ AL ABISMO.

> *(Then, the voices disappear just as suddenly as they came. **IVONNE** opens her eyes and is back in the desert with nobody but herself and the pink crosses that stand among her.)*

IVONNE. *(Mid-prayer.) Santa Maria, Madre de Dios,*

Ruega por nosotros, pecadores,

Ahora y en la hora de nuestra muerte,

Amen.

> *(She starts over.)*

Dios de salve Maria –

> *(Beat.)*

Wait.

How many was that?

>(*She counts the beads.*)

Shit.

I lost my fucking place.

Damn it this always happens. Why do they put so many goddamn beads on this stupid thing if –

(*To the sky.*) Perdoname Señor. I can't. There's no way of.

>(*Beat.*)

It's a lot of beads. That's all.

>(*Beat. She stands. For the first time, she notices how many crosses there are.*)

I don't remember there being this many of you.

>(*She reads a name on a cross. She knows exactly who this is. She traces the letters of a name with her fingertips.*)

>(**YOLANDA** *enters carrying an abundance of fliers. There is a picture on each one.*)

YOLANDA. *Discúlpe señora?*

Have you seen my –

>(**IVONNE** *is startled. She looks at* **YOLANDA**. *Dead silence. This lasts for an uncomfortably long time. Really, really, really long.*)

>(*Beat.*)

>(*Beat.*)

>(*Beat.*)

(Beat.)

(After a moment, **YOLANDA** *slaps* **IVONNE** *across the face. Hard.)*

*(***IVONNE*** *does not move.)*

*(***YOLANDA*** *slaps her again, even harder.)*

(Still, **IVONNE** *is motionless.)*

*(***YOLANDA*** *is about to go in for a third slap before* **IVONNE** *grabs* **YOLANDA** *by the wrist to stop her.* **YOLANDA** *pulls away.)*

What the / fuck are you doing here?

IVONNE. Yoli I was just passing / through –

YOLANDA. Don't say my name you selfish, selfish excuse for a woman.

You don't get to say my name not now not ever.

(A moment.)

Were you. Were you praying?

You were actually praying!

*(***YOLANDA*** *laughs. It starts off small but then builds to an uncontrollable, uncomfortable laughter.)*

(She continues to laugh. **IVONNE** *stands there, motionless.)*

IVONNE. I pray all the time, *Señora.*

YOLANDA. How strange.

IVONNE. Why's that?

YOLANDA. I don't know, you tell me.

(A moment.)

IVONNE. Yoli...

I'm not the / one –

YOLANDA. You were the last person to see / her.

IVONNE. I don't think I was, / actually.

YOLANDA. You took her to *El Centro* and she / didn't come back.

IVONNE. I didn't take her, she left / herself.

YOLANDA. You were the last person she was / with.

IVONNE. You don't know that for / sure.

YOLANDA. Don't tell me what I do and don't know.

I am her mother. I know everything.

(Beat.)

(Beat.)

(Beat.)

(Beat.)

IVONNE. You look good, Yoli. Time has been good to you.

YOLANDA. What are you doing here, Ivonne?

IVONNE. Picking up a couple of things I left / behind.

YOLANDA. I don't mean Juárez I mean here.

(Refers to the crosses.) What are you doing *here*.

IVONNE. What are *you* doing here, / huh?

YOLANDA. I get a lot of traction here, handing these out.

Your turn.

(Beat.)

IVONNE. I can give you a million reasons Yoli but none of them will ever be good enough so why even try.

YOLANDA. Because you owe me that much, that's why.

So you'd better try, you'd better fucking try.

(Explosive.) WHY ARE YOU HERE?!

IVONNE. To pay my respects.

To the...to...

I was hoping there'd be a cross for Brenda, / but...

YOLANDA. Say her name again and I will kill you myself.

IVONNE. She meant the world to me too / Yolanda.

YOLANDA. Lies, lies, lies, lies, lies, all you do is lie, it's like you can't / help it.

IVONNE. You have no idea what I've been through so / don't talk to me like you get me, okay?

YOLANDA. What you've been through? What YOU'VE been / through?

IVONNE. Yes what I'VE been through.

YOLANDA. You know what happened to her. You saw her last.

It's that simple. No other way around it.

> *(Beat.)*

The truth is coming out of you one way or another, Ivonne, even if it has to be squeezed out of you like water.

IVONNE. Is that a threat?

YOLANDA. *Es una promesa.*

IVONNE. I'm not afraid of *you*, *Señora.*

YOLANDA. I'm *not* the one you should be afraid of.

There are monsters out here in the desert, Ivonne.

IVONNE. ...

YOLANDA. Two years is a long time to just...disappear. Everybody's talking about it. About who you are, what you *owe*, what you *do*, / about why you left.

IVONNE. What do I do, *what do I DO*?

YOLANDA. And your little friends?

IVONNE. They're not my / friends.

YOLANDA. Word on the street is they're pissed. They want answers. They want / you.

IVONNE. You think you've got this whole thing figured out.

YOLANDA. I've got a pretty clear picture.

IVONNE. Okay so where's Brenda then, huh? If you've got a crystal clear image of how all this works then, please. *Explícamelo*. Where is she now?

> (**YOLANDA** *rushes* **IVONNE,** *tackles her to the ground. Straddles her and wraps her hands around her neck.*)

YOLANDA. Tell me where she is.

IVONNE. Yoli...

I can't...

No puedo respirar.

YOLANDA. Where is she.

IVONNE. I don't...

I don't...

YOLANDA. WHERE IS SHE DAMN IT?

IVONNE. I don't know!

YOLANDA. TELL ME!

IVONNE. It...it...

It was my family...or yours.

(**YOLANDA** *releases her.* **IVONNE** *coughs intensely.*)

YOLANDA. What?

IVONNE. It was my family or yours.

YOLANDA. No –

IVONNE. And if it were you, you would have done the same / thing.

YOLANDA. No. You're lying.

IVONNE. You know how this works, Yolanda, you know how *they* / work –

YOLANDA. (*Covering her ears.*) No, no, no, / no, no, no, no, no, no, no, no no no no no no –

IVONNE. Knowing where you live, who you talk to, who your *family is,* they will never stop until there's *nothing left,* as if you and the people around you never existed / in the first place!

YOLANDA. (*Ears still covered.*) La la la la / la la la la.

IVONNE. Open your ears and *listen* Yolanda, you wanna know the truth of it all so bad, then know it, because you can't *imagine* what they do, / nobody can!

YOLANDA. All I do is imagine, Ivonne. I'm alone. All the time, thinking and thinking and thinking and thinking, there's nothing you can say to me that I haven't already imagined myself, / NOTHING.

IVONNE. I WATCHED AS THREE MEN GRABBED HER AND PINNED HER TO THE GROUND!

(*Beat.*)

YOLANDA. Who? Pinned who to the ground, *mi Brendita*?

(**IVONNE** *is frozen.*)

Ivonne, who?

Who. Who. Who who who who –

IVONNE. *(Losing a piece of herself.)* My...sister...

    (Beat.)

YOLANDA. Erika?

    (IVONNE breaks.)

IVONNE. I...took too long this time.

YOLANDA. Oh Ivonne.

No. Oh no.

    (A moment.)

    (IVONNE pulls it together for a moment. She is very still. This is very still.)

IVONNE. One of them ripped off her favorite blouse with his hands. I gave it to her on her birthday, it was white. The other one grabbed a plastic bag from the trash can. I could barely see her eyes. They looked me straight in the eyes and said "this is what you get for being a bad girl, you get to watch."

He pulled down her pants, he spit, he shoved, he...

I could feel my skin my fingernails clawing deeper and deeper into the bedpost trying to scream trying to help but they tied me the other side of the room so I couldn't stop them.

There was a curling iron sitting, sitting on the...

I've never heard a scream like that before.

Next thing I know, we're in the back of a van. It's blue. We drive for awhile before the back door swings open and I can feel the breeze and the hot summer sun and like a pile of trash, they throw her body in the desert, slam the door shut, and drive off.

They dropped me off at the S-Mart by the bridge. And told me to call them when I got home.

(Beat.)

But I went to your house instead. I wanted to tell you, wanted to scream, wanted to take you with me, away from here, away from all this but I was scared.

*(**YOLANDA** reaches for her. **IVONNE** pulls away.)*

I needed you to be there for me. I needed a mother. I don't have anyone else.

YOLANDA. *(Tender.)* I couldn't protect you, Ivonne, not from this. If they were using Erika to get you to...there's no way I could have.

IVONNE. But you can tackle me, threaten me, throw me out into the street and feel pretty good about all that?

You think because you know the truth now that you can walk away, start over, start fresh, well it doesn't work like that Yolanda because you still don't even know the half of it. Trust me. You don't. I know what it's like to have someone ripped from your arms, Erika was *my* everything. So don't go trying to fix this, trying to tell me what you could or could not do because *I'VE* LIVED A LIFE OF FEAR AND PAIN AND I WILL DROWN YOU IN IT! I WILL FLOOD THIS ENTIRE DESERT WITH IT!

(A moment.)

I'm not the monsters who took your daughter, *Señora.* As much as you'd like me to be? ...I'm not.

(Beat.)

(Beat.)

(Beat.)

(Beat.)

YOLANDA. *(On the verge.)* I can't live my life thinking that something like that happened to *mi Brendita*, Ivonne.

So I'm asking you. Please.

If you know. Tell me.

Where is my daughter?

Please. Please.

IVONNE. I wish I knew.

(Lights shift.)

Eight
A Woman Burned is a Woman Scorned

(Projections: **MONDAY JULY 6, 1998. ONE DAY BEFORE BRENDA'S DISAPPEARANCE.***)*

*(***BRENDA** *and* **IVONNE** *sitting on the living room floor of* **BRENDA***'s home. Tejano music blasts from a boom box nearby. It's fun and buoyant. Maybe, perhaps, something like Selena*.)*

(The two sit braiding each other's hair, laughing and conversing.)

IVONNE. *(Sing-song.)* You like him.

BRENDA. I do not!

IVONNE. I see the way you talk to him.

"Hola Marquitos."

BRENDA. *Ya callate!* I don't sound like that.

*(***IVONNE** *shoots* **BRENDA** *a look.)*

Okay, maybe a little.

I don't know how to talk to him.

IVONNE. *Ay niña!* You talk to him like you talk to me. Don't you trust your *tia Ivonne*?

BRENDA. It's not the same. And you're not my tia.

IVONNE. Shit might as well be. How many times has Yolanda called me all nice and sweet like "Can you

---

* A license to produce *La Ruta* does not include a performance license for any third-party or copyrighted music. Licensees should create an original composition or use music in the public domain. For further information, please see the Music and Third Party Materials Use Note on page iii.

please come and look after Brenda while I run a few errands?"

BRENDA. She treats me like I'm a kid. I'm sixteen, I can take care of / myself.

IVONNE. Uh huh oh yes Miss Independent over here can stay home alone but can't talk to pimple face Marquitos!

BRENDA. He does not have a pimple face! He has a cute face.

IVONNE. You do like him!!

BRENDA. *(Buries her face in her hands.)* Okay fine, *ya*! My cheeks get so red I can't even look at him. I almost pressed my hand in one of the machines 'cause he cut his hair and looked so adorable with the little flat top.

IVONNE. We get it, we get it. You're into him.

So. Do you wanna learn how to talk to him or not? 'Cause I can leave if you want.

BRENDA. Okay...but if you tell anyone –

IVONNE. Who am I gonna tell?

BRENDA. Uh let's see: Sylvia, Navil, Natali, Maydaly –

IVONNE. Ew, I don't even talk to those *putas*.

BRENDA. That doesn't matter. You have the biggest mouth in all of the *maquilas* and you know it.

IVONNE. But this is between us sisters. A pact. You have my word. *Bueno.* Come here *chiquita*.

(She does.)

Okay. Pretend I'm Marcos. Now...talk to me.

BRENDA. Okay. Okay.

(She takes in a deep breath. A la awkward:)

Hola Marquitos.

IVONNE. *(Deep voice; a la Marquitos.)* Hola Brenda.

BRENDA. Ivonne, this is stupid.

IVONNE. What? He's got a deep voice!

BRENDA. You sound nothing like him!

IVONNE. *(Laughing.)* I'm sorry, I'm sorry. Okay forget the voice. *Otra vez, otra vez...*

BRENDA. No.

IVONNE. *Hechale ganas!* Come on!

> *(A moment.)*

What's your favorite song?

BRENDA. What does that have to do / with –

IVONNE. Thinking of something familiar will loosen you up a bit.

So your favorite song. What is it?

BRENDA. *(Thinking fast.)* Uh I don't know.

"La Bruja," I guess.

> *(IVONNE looks confused.)*

Have you not heard of –

IVONNE. Everyone's heard of "La Bruja."

Whenever you get nervous around him, take a deep breath and think of...

(Trying not to laugh.) "La Bruja."

> *(A moment. BRENDA closes her eyes, takes a deep breath, and thinks of "La Bruja.")*

BRENDA. *Hola Marcos. Soy Brenda.*

IVONNE. *A la chingada!* You see? Was that so hard?

> *(IVONNE's phone rings. She doesn't answer.)*

BRENDA. Aren't you gonna get that?

IVONNE. If it's important they'll call back.

> *(She ties the end of* **BRENDA**'*s braid.)*

Wait one second...

> *(She searches the room for something.)*

You know, sometimes I forget the only thing between our beds and the desert is a thin layer of concrete.

> *(She picks a flower from the corner of the living room floor and shoves it in* **BRENDA**'*s braid.)*

BRENDA. *(Re: the flower in her hair.)* It's a little tight, no?

IVONNE. It's perfect.

> *(A moment.)*

Ay que bonita. Now you look like Desamaya.

BRENDA. The singer?

IVONNE. *La Reina de Juárez.*

BRENDA. God I love her voice.

IVONNE. Me too.

BRENDA. I wish I could sing like that.

IVONNE. That sound... I can count on one hand how many people can sing like that. *Chavela Vargas, Lola Beltran...y Desamaya.* These women...their voices are of the earth. You've had to have been through some shit to sound like that.

> *(Beat.)*

She's coming back to Juárez at the end of her tour. Erika and I are going. You should come! I'll get an extra ticket, it'll be fun.

(Beat.)

BRENDA. You don't know.

IVONNE. Don't know what?

BRENDA. She uh... Died? Passed away? She got... / Was killed?

IVONNE. But she's on tour.

BRENDA. Yeah. She was.

IVONNE. But I was gonna –

Erika really wanted to –

(A moment.)

BRENDA. It just happened. Like. Two days ago, or something.

(A moment.)

Her tour bus got shot up near *Campo Algodonero* as they were heading out of town... And then somebody kidnapped her... It's like, she's already dead, why would you wanna kidnap her?

IVONNE. She wasn't kidnapped, she was taken. You have to be alive to be kidnapped.

(Beat.)

BRENDA. I can't believe you didn't hear about this.

IVONNE. No, I...somehow missed that.

BRENDA. Yeah...that's why they keep playing her songs on *la radio.*

IVONNE. A woman kept alive by the sound of her voice.

BRENDA. My mom cries every time she comes on now.

*(Beat. **IVONNE** looks on, in a daze.)*

(Referring to her hair.) Want me to do yours?

IVONNE. Uh sure. Why not.

> (*She sits in front of* **BRENDA** *and loosens her hair.*)

BRENDA. Ugh I swear if I have to hear about Maya's breakups one more time...

IVONNE. I know right? It's so annoying.

> (**IVONNE**'s *phone rings again.*)

BRENDA. You're very popular today.

IVONNE. It's probably Raúl. I'll call him later.

Anyway. What were we talking about? Oh right. *Pinche Maya* dude I swear the *maquila* is worse than high school.

BRENDA. You know *mi mamá* still tries to convince me to quit? The other night I had blisters on my feet this big and she asked if she could help me soak them, right? So she sat there and massaged my feet for like an hour and she wouldn't stop crying. I think she feels bad about the whole thing.

> (*The phone rings again.*)
>
> (**IVONNE** *takes the phone, opens it, and hangs it up.*)
>
> (*A moment.*)
>
> (*Then.*)
>
> (*The phone rings again.*)
>
> (**IVONNE** *answers.*)

IVONNE. (*Yelling in the phone.*) Stop fucking calling me!

> (*She hangs up.*)

Fuck.

BRENDA. Ivonne...

What's going on? Is everything okay?

(**IVONNE** *gags.*)

IVONNE. Oh my God.

(*She gags again.*)

I think I'm gonna throw up.

BRENDA. Oh, no. Um, there's a trash can over there, please not on the floor.

(**IVONNE** *rushes over to the trash can.*)

(*She tries to throw up but nothing comes out.*)

Was it something you ate?

(**IVONNE**'s *phone rings again.*)

(*She answers it again.*)

IVONNE. WHAT WHAT WHAT.

(*A moment.*)

(*Quiet.*) I know.

(*A moment.*)

I know.

(*A long moment.*)

Got it.

Bye.

(*Beat.*)

(*Beat.*)

(*Beat.*)

(Beat.)

Listen. Um.

What are you doing tomorrow?

BRENDA. Should I call *mi mamá*? You don't looks so / good.

IVONNE. I'm fine *chiquita,* acid reflux from lunch, *pinche Menudo.*

What are you doing tomorrow?

BRENDA. I, uh. I'm working at the *maquila* and then / I –

IVONNE. Skip.

BRENDA. What?

IVONNE. Skip. Let's hang out.

BRENDA. Ivonne I can't walk out like that I have a job.

IVONNE. Oh come on! We can get our nails done...go to the movies... Peter Piper. My treat. Like a girls night out.

> *(Beat.)*

BRENDA. You'd do all that? For me?

IVONNE. I'll talk to José. He always listens to me. What do you say?

> *(A moment.)*

BRENDA. You *sure* José will be cool with it.

IVONNE. Oh yeah. Just. Don't tell your mom. If anyone gets us in trouble, it'll be Yolanda.

> *(Beat.)*

BRENDA. Okay. Let's do it!

IVONNE. *Eso!* We can meet at this cute little shoe store in *El Centro.* Have you heard of this place? It's called

Gerardos. They've got shoes there from all over the world.

BRENDA. *Imagínate.*

IVONNE. Always a mandatory first stop on a girls night out. We'll get you something cute, too.

BRENDA. Okay!

IVONNE. Meet me there around six. It's the one closest to the bridge, right next to *Piñeda?* You can't miss it.

BRENDA. Ahhh!!!! So exciting!!!

IVONNE. Yeah. Exciting.

Bueno. I should probably head home before it gets too dark. Tell Yoli I left that *crema* she wanted in her bathroom. It smells like heaven. *Buenas noches, pequeña.*

(*She kisses* BRENDA's *cheeks.*)

BRENDA. *Buenas noches.*

(IVONNE *heads out.*)

(*She throws up in a bush outside.*)

(*Lights shift.*)

Nine
Ni Una Más and Swallowing Deserts

(Projections: **WEDNESDAY AUGUST 23, 2000.
TWO YEARS AND FORTY-SEVEN DAYS AFTER
BRENDA'S DISAPPEARANCE. 1:13 P.M.***)*

(El Centro, Ciudad Juárez, México.)

*(The low roar of women chanting "Ni Una
Más" can be heard from a distance. It grows
and grows and grows.)*

(Lights rise **MARISELA** *standing alone, firm,
wearing a handmade poster of a missing
young woman like a dress.)*

*(Above, below, and around the image, it
reads:
Rubí Marisol.
16 años. Q.E.P.D.
Justicia. Justicia.
Para El Asesino.
Pena Máxima.)*

*(She has red lipstick smeared big around
and on her lips. Her nose is painted red. Tear
drops are etched on her cheeks – still wet.
Probably from cheap eyeliner.)*

(She looks like a clown.)

*(The chanting builds and builds till it
crescendos to a haltering stop.)*

MARISELA. *Mujeres!*

Three hundred and sixty-six kilometers stand between
the Chihuahua State Capital and Juárez. This journey
is not an easy one. Thorns will pierce through your feet

and the Mexican authorities will retaliate with a force as strong as the wind.

And you will feel thirsty. And weak. And tired.

But remember...pink crosses stand in the place of women who aren't here anymore. Hundreds of young girls in Juárez dead. Thousands more still missing. Nipples are being bitten off and worn around the necks of men in the shadows whose faces we can't even see *nomas por ser mujeres*!

Señoras por favor escuchenme! I am angry. I am heartbroken. But the heart of a woman beats furiously in a million directions at once, even when it's shattered into a million pieces. It is okay to be scared. I am. But then I think of *mi hija* and I think of all of you and I remember why we're here.

So let us paint pink crosses and wear their pictures like dresses, *mujeres*, because we can never stop...until the desert stops swallowing our girls!

> *(An uproar of cheers from all over.)*

> *(Then, in a quickness,* **YOLANDA** *appears from the shadows, wearing an old zip-up sweater hoodie type of thing, with a graphic T-shirt peeking out from inside. Something iconically American like GAP or Aéropostale or Hollister, and a pair of ill-fitted jeans.)*

> *(They stare at each other for awhile. A long, long while.)*

> *(Beat.)*

> *(Beat.)*

> *(Beat.)*

> *(Beat.)*

YOLANDA. Nice speech.

MARISELA. Thanks.

YOLANDA. Did someone help you write that, / or...?

MARISELA. I wrote it myself.

YOLANDA. Since when do you talk like that?

MARISELA. Since always.

YOLANDA. No. Not since always. I've never heard you talk like that.

(*Beat. A moment.*)

What's with the makeup?

MARISELA. It's part of the show. I'm in character.

YOLANDA. What...*character*?

MARISELA. *Como Shakespeare.*

YOLANDA. Uh huh.

MARISELA. For the protest. The march.

YOLANDA. You wanna get yourself killed? Is that what this is?

MARISELA. Yeah, you don't get it.

YOLANDA. No, I get it. I just think it's stupid, that's all.

MARISELA. Got it.

YOLANDA. *Como una payasa.*

MARISELA. *Fue un teatro, Yolanda y los payasos somos la familia de las victimas.* We <u>are</u> the clowns. So, yeah. I thought I'd play the part.

YOLANDA. This isn't funny, Marisela. As much as you try to pretend like you're Wonder Woman you're not. *No eres más que una mujer, dejalo ya.*

MARISELA. And do what instead? Wait around? Hand out fliers?

YOLANDA. Better than *this*.

MARISELA. And how's that working out for you?

(*Beat.*)

YOLANDA. You know, just 'cause I haven't spent the last two years with these <u>locas</u> / in the street causing all types of noise doesn't mean I'm doing it wrong.

MARISELA. They're not *locas Yolanda*, stop calling / them that!

No one says you're doing it wrong, I never said that!

YOLANDA. Every day you're out here with these women is one day closer to your grave. Is that what you want?

MARISELA. I want to feel *something* Yolanda. *That's* what I want.

YOLANDA. And when does that happen?

MARISELA. When our daughters can come home safe, without worry.

YOLANDA. Well then you must have some brilliant plan to save all the women in Juárez so please. *Dale.* I'm listening.

(*Beat.*)

MARISELA. *No se.*

YOLANDA. *Exactamente.*

(*Beat. A moment.*)

(*Hurt. Shocked.*) I don't even recognize you anymore.

MARISELA. Yeah, well. Me neither.

(*A moment.*)

YOLANDA. Marisela...

Ivonne's back. She...she came back.

MARISELA. What? That's...that's not possible.

YOLANDA. I bumped into her at *Campo Algodonero.*

I was doing my rounds and she was... She was praying, can you believe it? There she was and I I I I think she might know. I think she might know where Brenda is, or at least have an idea.

(*Beat.*)

I'm not crazy Marisela.

MARISELA. I know you're not.

YOLANDA. Stop looking at me like I am.

(*Beat. Careful.*)

MARISELA. She's been gone two years, Yoli.

YOLANDA. I know how long it's been.

MARISELA. Then you should also know that the longer Brenda is gone / the less likely it is that she's even in one piece.

YOLANDA. No what I know, is that Brenda left for work, she got on *la ruta* and / she hasn't come back –

MARISELA. *Ya* with *la ruta, Yolanda*! You make it sound like it's some vacuum swallowing everything in its path / and it's not, it's a *pinche* bus!

YOLANDA. Because that's what it is!

MARISELA. It's *not* just *la ruta* it's everything! Look around you! Everything is entangled!

It's not just the boyfriends or the bus routes, it's the *narcos,* it's the police, it's the government, it's the newspapers, the *maquilas,* the *borrachos, los hombres de Juárez, los padres tambien, ES TODO*! We are

ALWAYS on *la ruta, Yolanda, y ya mero,* it's time to get off.

(Beat.)

Join us. March with us. From Juárez to Chihuahua. We are going to set up a *permanent protest* right in front of the Chihuahua State Capital until they fix this mess. This is your chance to *do something.* So do it. Do it for Brenda.

YOLANDA. Brenda needs me to stay here, to wait for her *here.*

MARISELA. You need to let her go.

YOLANDA. She's not dead *maldita sea*! Going to Chihuahua makes her dead and she's not dead she's not!

(Beat.)

(A moment.)

MARISELA. Going to Chihuahua keeps her *alive.* It keeps her alive, it does.

(A moment.)

I know what it's like to want something, anything, to prove that she's dead or alive, that it's real or that it's not. But either way...waiting around won't do a thing. They call us *las locas de Juárez*...but we're not. Don't give into it. Come with us. Fight back.

YOLANDA. But we have a chance here Mari!

Because Ivonne's back, / Ivonne's –

MARISELA. Ivonne's dead.

They found her body by the pink crosses a couple of hours ago.

They got to her, Yoli. They got to her first.

(The crowd starts chanting "NI UNA MÁS.")

YOLANDA. No   no no no no no no no no
no no no no no no no

   I think I'm gonna   I think / I'm gonna be sick.

MARISELA. *(Noticing the momentum of the crowd.)* We
   have to go. Now.

         (Beat. A moment.)

YOLANDA. *(Near tears.)* I can't.

         *(The chanting sits at a low, low roar – as it
         travels further and further away from them.)*

         (**MARISELA** *walks over to* **YOLANDA** *and
         embraces her. It's long overdue and is full
         of so much past, so much present. All the
         in-betweens are laced in this very moment.)*

         (Beat.)

         (Beat.)

         (Beat.)

         (Beat.)

         (A prophecy.)

MARISELA. They will follow me all the way to Chihuahua...

   I'll receive death threats every step of the way.

YOLANDA. By the time you get there...

MARISELA. They'll kill me.

YOLANDA. They'll kill you.

MARISELA. Some random guy will just...walk right up to
   me...in the middle of the day...as I'm steps away from

pulling the door open...and shoot me dead. Right there. On the steps of the court. And get away with it.

They will kill me this time.

And then they will kill my family.

And then they will kill everyone who testifies on my behalf in court.

And then three thousand more women after me.

And thousands more all over the world.

Across the border.

In every city.

I'm sure of it.

>*(Beat. A moment.)*

But I *have* to do this.

This is my ministry.

>*(A moment.)*

I love you.

>*(Beat.)*

>*(Beat.)*

>*(Beat.)*

>*(Beat.)*

YOLANDA. *Que Dios de bendiga.*

>*(And just like that, they're all gone.)*

>*(YOLANDA is left standing in the middle of the desert – alone.)*

(Alone with her thoughts, with her prayers, with her memories.)

(The sound of the wind against the hot, coarse desert sand. Just like the time before. We sit in this for awhile.)

(Then.)

(Several hours later.)

(The wind against the desert sand turns into a tune of some kind. The breathiness of the wind turns into the breath of a woman. The faint sound of percussion and the strum of a guitar that can only be heard in the depths of the desert find its way to this breath. A sound both painfully unreal, and hauntingly familiar all at once.)

(Is it music? Is it the sun? Is it the wind? Perhaps it is neither. Perhaps it is all of the above.)

(The sounds of the desert turn into song. **YOLANDA** *closes her eyes and is swallowed by its rhythm. She hears a voice and a familiar tune unfold. The voice she hears sounds a lot like* **DESAMAYA.***)*

(The song itself a song she's heard a million times before, except this time...something is different about it. It's haunting. A warning. A reminder. A conjuring.)

[VI. "LA BRUJA – REVISITED"]

DESAMAYA.

¡AY QUÉ BONITO ES VOLAR
A LAS DOS DE LA MAÑANA

A LAS DOS DE LA MAÑANA
AY QUÉ BONITO ES VOLAR, AY MAMÁ!

VOLAR Y DEJARSE CAER,
EN LOS BRAZOS DE UNA DAMA,
¡AY QUÉ BONITO ES VOLAR
EN LOS BRAZOS DE TU HERMANA, AY MAMÁ!

> *(And just like that, the Women of Juárez appear in the middle of the desert, in the middle of* **YOLANDA***'s memories. They sing, and she listens. She listens closely now. Words she's heard a million times before, but has never really understood them...until now.)*

BRENDA & DESAMAYA.
ME AGARRA LA BRUJA,
ME LLEVA A SU CASA,
ME VUELVE MACETA,
Y UNA CALABAZA

ALL.
ME AGARRA LA BRUJA,
ME LLEVA AL CERRITO,
ME VUELVE MACETA,
Y UN CALABACITO

DESAMAYA.
¡AY! DÍGAME, Y DÍGAME, Y DÍGAME USTED?
¿CUANTÁS CRIATURITAS SE HA CHUPADO USTED?
NINGUNA, NINGUNA, NINGUNA NO SÉ,
QUE ANDO EN PRETENSIONES DE CHUPARME A USTED

> *(The women look at* **YOLANDA.** *Expectingly. Curiously. Encouragingly.)*

> *(Does she hear their song? Can she sing it too? Maybe faces of real missing women are projected onto the walls. A moment. Then.)*

YOLANDA.

> ¡AY! ME ESPANTÓ UNA MUJER
> EN MEDIO DEL MAR SALADO
> EN MEDIO DEL MAR SALADO
> ¡AY ME ESPANTÓ UNA MUJER, AY MAMÁ!
> PORQUE NO QUERÍA CREER
> LO QUÉ ME HABÍAN CONTADO
> LO DE ARRIBA ERA MUJER
> Y LO DE ABAJO PESCADO ¡AY MAMÁ!

YOLANDA, DESAMAYA & IVONNE.

> LEVÁNTATE HERMANA

YOLANDA, DESAMAYA & IVONNE (ADD BRENDA).

> LEVÁNTATE MIJA
> AHÍ VIENE LA BRUJA
> DETRÁS DE TU TÍA

YOLANDA, DESAMAYA, IVONNE & BRENDA (ADD ZAIDE).

> LEVÁNTATE OBRERA,

YOLANDA, DESAMAYA, IVONNE, BRENDA, ZAIDE, (ADD MARISELA) & ALL.

> LEVÁNTATE MÁMA,
> QUE AHÍ ANDA LA BRUJA
> NOS DEJA SIN NADA
>
> ¡AY DÍGAME, Y DÍGAME, Y DÍGAME USTED!
> ¿CUANTÁS CRIATURITAS SE HA CHUPADO USTED?
> NINGUNA, NINGUNA, NINGUNA NO VÉ, QUE
> ANDO EN PRETENSIONES DE CHUPARME A USTED.

> *(The guitar crescendos until suddenly, the music stops, and the sand comes crashing down, and the women stand tall and strong like pink crosses in the desert.)*

> *(We're back to reality.)*

> *(**YOLANDA** stares at the mound of sand before her, catching her breath.)*

(Beat.)

(Beat.)

(Beat.)

(Beat.)

They call us *las locas de Juárez...*

but we're not.

*(**YOLANDA** takes a handful of sand...)*

(And slowly shoves it in her mouth. She eats it. Slowly and efficiently.)

(Then, another handful.)

(She eats.)

(And eats.)

(And eats.)

End of Play

Son del Obrero

Huapango Norteño
♩. = 116

by Gabino Palomares

Guitar strums straight eighth notes throughout, except as noted last section.
For each entrance, guitar vamps usually 4 bars,
then DESAMAYA sings first, with any others joining on the echo.

cue: "...go back!"

Tra - ba - ja - do - ra er - es

tú, tra - ba - ja - do - ra tam-bién yo._____ 1.Tra -
2.Si

se - gui - mos se - pa - ra - das nun - ca ha -

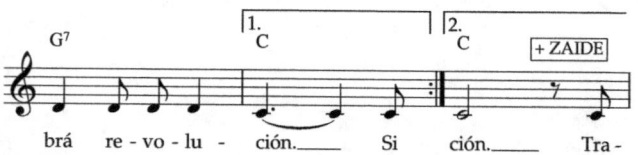

brá re - vo - lu - ción._____ Si ción._____ Tra -

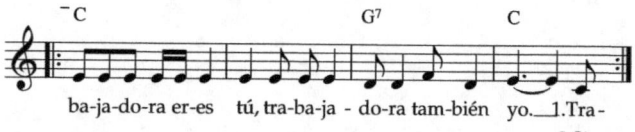

ba-ja-do-ra er-es tú, tra-ba-ja - do-ra tam-bién yo.__1.Tra -
2.Si

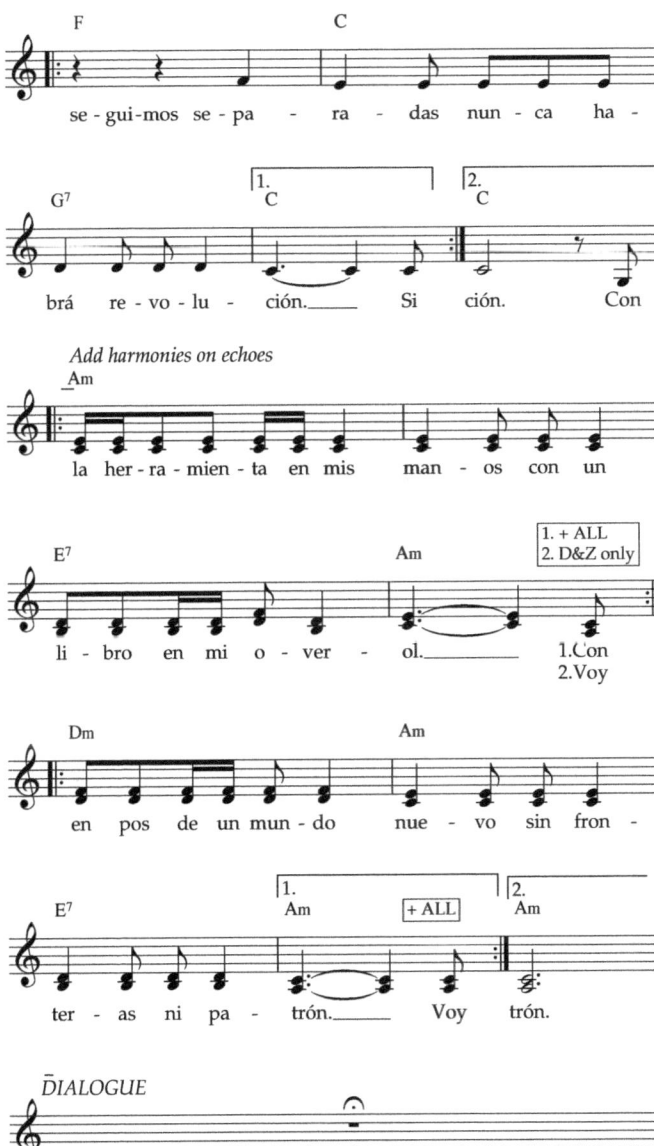

se - gui-mos se - pa - ra - das nun - ca ha -

1. C
brá re - vo - lu - ción._____ Si ción.

2. C
Con

Add harmonies on echoes

la her - ra - mien - ta en mis man - os con un

li - bro en mi o - ver - ol._____

1. + ALL
2. D&Z only

1.Con
2.Voy

en pos de un mun - do nue - vo sin fron -

1. Am
+ ALL
ter - as ni pa - trón._____ Voy

2. Am
trón.

DIALOGUE

Guitar cue: *"...you don't know shit!"*
Vocal cue: *"...try this thing or what?"*

ba-ja-do-ra er-es   tú, tra-ba-ja - do-ra tam-bién yo.___ 1.Tra
                                                                                      2.Si

se - gui - mos se - pa - - - - ra - - - das nun - ca ha -

brá re-vo-lu - ción.___   Si   ción._____

DIALOGUE

cue: "Water isn't worth it."

DESAMAYA

pp   Muy   pron - to el pro - le - tar -

ia - do con la   ra - zón ven-cer - á.___ 1.Muy
                                                                2.Los

pro-duc-tos del tra - ba - jo del tra - ba - ja - dor se -
f

DIALOGUE

Tired
♩ = 120

DESAMAYA only on the first line. On echo, add all except ZAIDE. Others drop out gradually as they leave the bus, until only DESAMAYA is left singing at the end.

mp Tra

Am

ba - ja - do - ra er - es tú, tra - ba - ja -

Am

dor - a tam - bién yo. 1.Tra -
2.Si

E⁷   Am

se - gui - mos se - pa - ra - das nun - ca ha -

Dm   Am

Siete Soles

by Rafael Mendoza

Cardenche ♩. = 50

Sung a cappella. Chords provided for rehearsal only.
Rhythm is sung very freely, wth Desamaya leading.

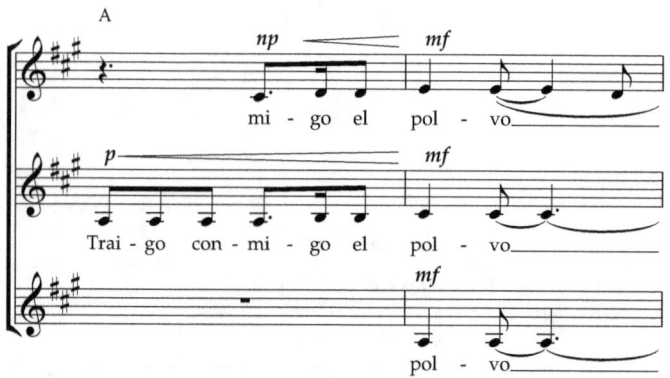

A

np ———— *mf*
mi - go el pol - vo_____

p ———————— *mf*
Trai - go con - mi - go el pol - vo_____

mf
pol - vo_____

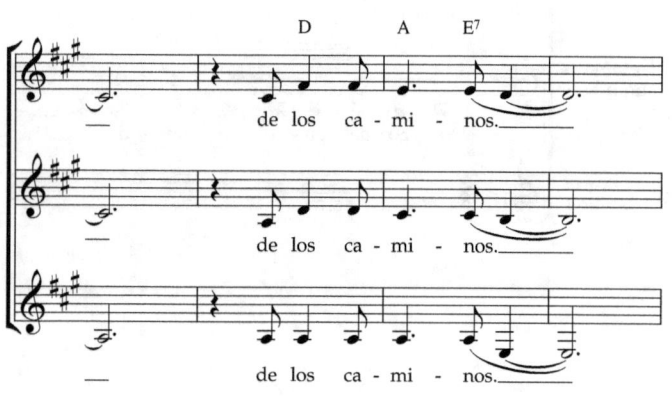

D   A   E⁷

_____ de los ca - mi - nos._____

_____ de los ca - mi - nos._____

_____ de los ca - mi - nos._____

Bm   D

Ya no me que - da na - da,_____

Ya no me que - da na - da,_____

Ya no me que - da na - da,_____

to - do lo sé per - di - do,_____

to - do lo sé per - di - do,_____

to - do lo sé per - di - do,_____

di-cen que a-lláen el nor - te es-tá mi des - ti - no.____

di-cen que a-lláen el nor - te es-tá mi des - ti - no.____

di-cen que a-lláen el nor - te es-tá mi des - ti - no.____

ra - yos____

Me en-can-di-lan los ra - yos____

yos____

de sie - te so - - - les.

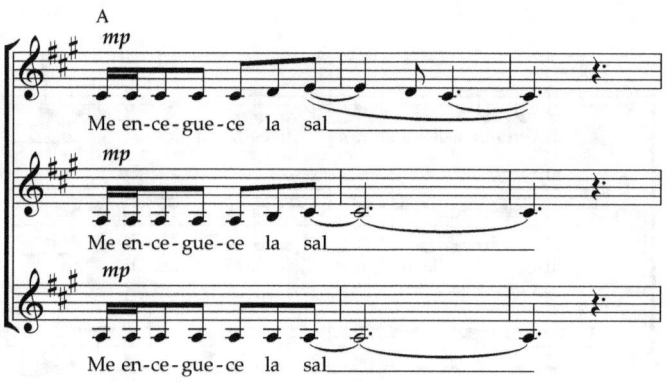

Me en - ce - gue - ce la sal_____

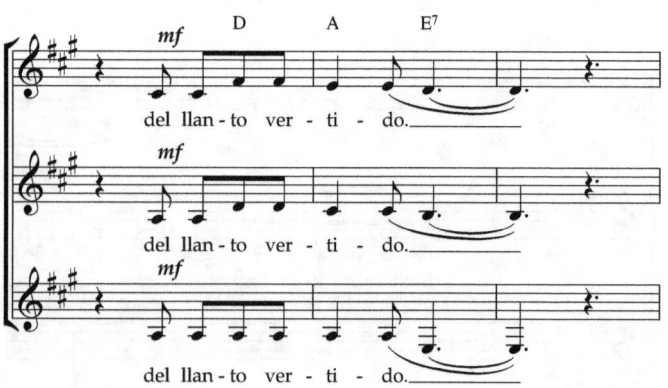

del llan - to ver - ti - do._____

D   *f*   *sub. p*

Ya na - da me de - tie - ne,_____

f   *sub. p*

Ya na - da me de - tie - ne,_____ *sub. p*

f

Ya na - da me de - tie - ne,_____

A

ya me ves - tí de ol - vi - do,

ya me ves - tí de ol - vi - do,

ya me ves - tí de ol - vi - do,

E⁷   A

mp

mi des -

mp

su - pe que a-lláen el nor - te es - tá mi des -

mp

nor - te es - tá mi des -

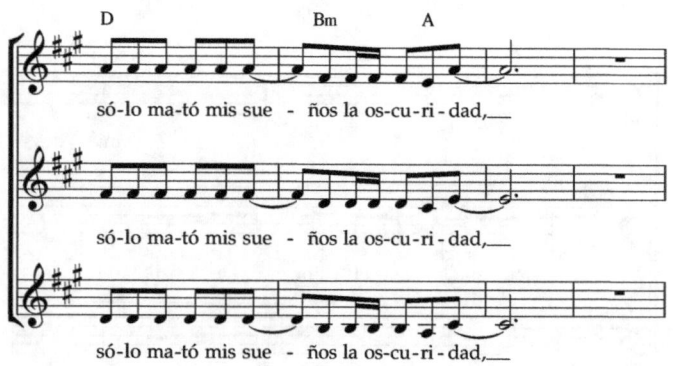

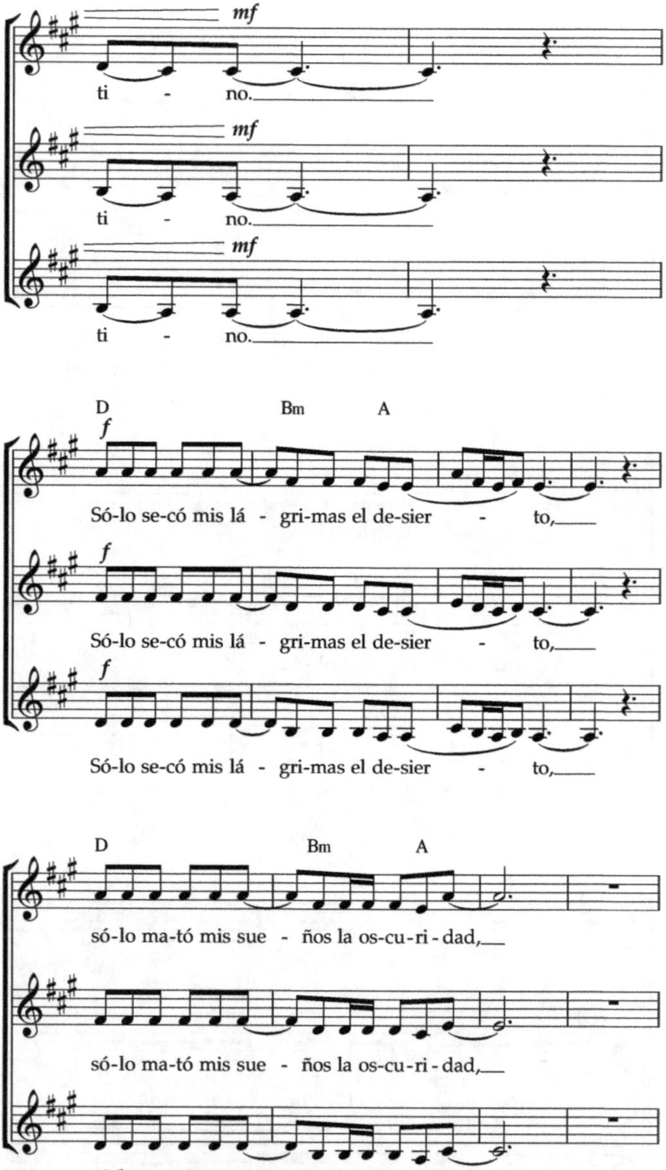

mf
ti - no.
mf
ti - no.
mf
ti - no.
D Bm A
f
Só-lo se-có mis lá - gri-mas el de-sier - to,
f
Só-lo se-có mis lá - gri-mas el de-sier - to,
f
Só-lo se-có mis lá - gri-mas el de-sier - to,
D Bm A
só-lo ma-tó mis sue - ños la os-cu-ri-dad,
só-lo ma-tó mis sue - ños la os-cu-ri-dad,
só-lo ma-tó mis sue - ños la os-cu-ri-dad,

só-lo se-guí el des-te - llo de un es-pe - jis-mo,_____

só-lo se-guí el des-te - llo de un es-pe - jis-mo,_____

só-lo se-guí el des-te - llo de un es-pe - jis-mo,_____

ba - jo los sie - te so - les_____

ba - jo los sie - te so - les_____

ba - jo los sie - te so - les_____

caí al a - bis - mo.

caí al a - bis - mo.

caí al a - bis - mo.

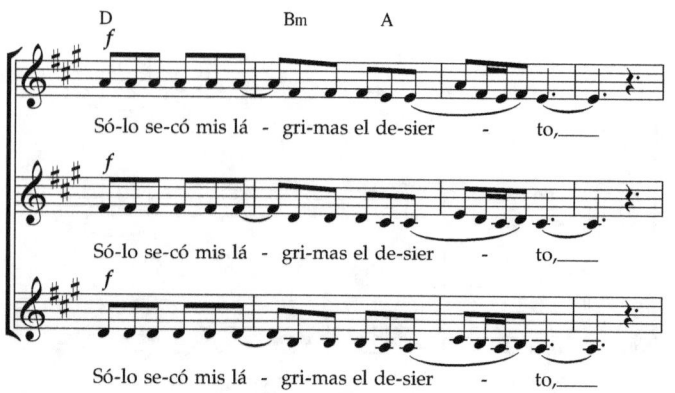

Só-lo se-có mis lá - gri-mas el de-sier - to,___

Só-lo se-có mis lá - gri-mas el de-sier - to,___

Só-lo se-có mis lá - gri-mas el de-sier - to,___

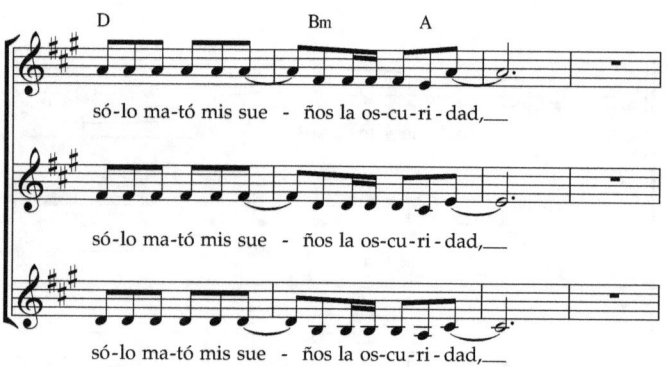

só-lo ma-tó mis sue - ños la os-cu-ri-dad,___

só-lo ma-tó mis sue - ños la os-cu-ri-dad,___

só-lo ma-tó mis sue - ños la os-cu-ri-dad,___

só-lo se-guí el des-te - llo de un es-pe - jis-mo,___

só-lo se-guí el des-te - llo de un es-pe - jis-mo,___

só-lo se-guí el des-te - llo de un es-pe - jis-mo,___

A · *mp*

ba - jo los sie - te so - les_____

mp

ba - jo los sie - te so - les_____

mp

ba - jo los sie-te so - les_____

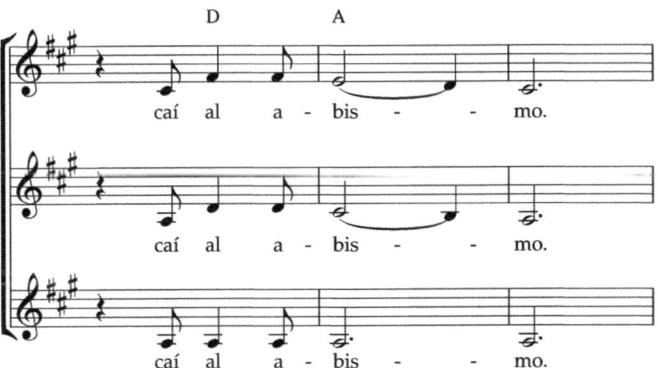

D · A

caí al a - bis - - mo.

caí al a - bis - - mo.

caí al a - bis - - mo.

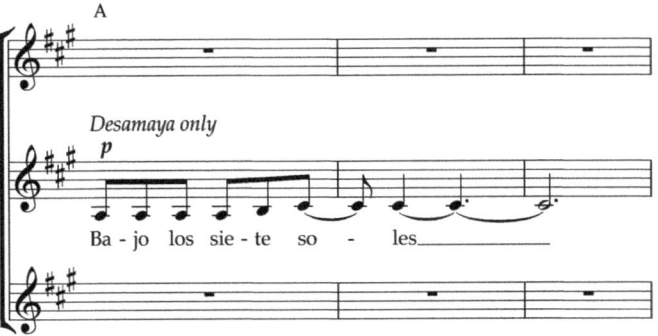

A

Desamaya only
p

Ba - jo los sie - te so - les_____

caí al a - bis - mo._____